"Dance with me, Catherine," Miles commanded her softly.

She went on leaden feet, knowing that to refuse would be childish, like backing down from a dare. Then the music changed from the frenetic beat of the lambada to a soft ballad. Catherine smiled and stopped, a few steps from the dance floor. "Music's changed. Well, that's that—"

"No, it's not." He spun her into his arms and walked her onto the floor. "We'll just have to dance slow."

She was helpless to do anything else. Her body was pressed against his, hip to hip and chest to chest. His hand was at the small of her back, pulling her closer still.

Every inch of her body was aware of every inch of his, every sense aware of his breath against her hair . . . his scent intoxicating her, his mouth there for the tasting. . . .

She had been terrified to dance the blatant lambada with him, but this was much worse. The lambada was all sex and no tenderness. But in Miles's arms, she felt as if they were making love in front of everyone—slowly prolonging their passion in a test of control, before a wild burst of ecstasy erupted.

"You feel so right," he murmured. "I knew you would. . . ."

WHAT ARE *LOVESWEPT* ROMANCES?

They are stories of true romance and touching emotion. We believe those two very important ingredients are constants in our highly sensual and very believable stories in the *LOVESWEPT* line. Our goal is to give you, the reader, stories of consistently high quality that may sometimes make you laugh, sometimes make you cry, but are always fresh and creative and contain many delightful surprises within their pages.

Most romance fans read an enormous number of books. Those they truly love, they keep. Others may be traded with friends and soon forgotten. We hope that each *LOVESWEPT* romance will be a treasure—a "keeper." We will always try to publish

LOVE STORIES YOU'LL NEVER FORGET
BY AUTHORS YOU'LL ALWAYS REMEMBER

The Editors

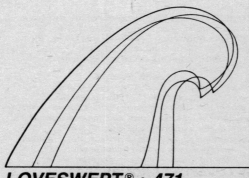

LOVESWEPT® · 471
Linda Cajio
Earth Angel

 BANTAM BOOKS
NEW YORK · TORONTO · LONDON · SYDNEY · AUCKLAND

EARTH ANGEL

A Bantam Book / May 1991

If you would be interested in receiving protective vinyl
covers for your Loveswept books, please write to this address
for information:

Loveswept
Bantam Books
P.O. Box 985
Hicksville, NY 11802

ISBN 0-553-44117-5

Published simultaneously in the United States and Canada

Bantam Books are published by Bantam Books, a division
of Bantam Doubleday Dell Publishing Group, Inc. Its trademark, consisting of the words "Bantam Books" and the
portrayal of a rooster, is Registered in U.S. Patent and
Trademark Office and in other countries. Marca Registrada.
Bantam Books, 666 Fifth Avenue, New York, New York
10103.

PRINTED IN THE UNITED STATES OF AMERICA

OPM 0 9 8 7 6 5 4 3 2 1

Many thanks to LINC for all its collective brains, and to Dot Brown for "Earth Angel." I love the song too. Let's keep the earth green and growing. It's all we've got.

One

"Are you going to throw that away?"

Miles Kitteridge stopped in mid-toss, the paper still crumpled in his hand. His office door had been flung open with a bang, and standing on the threshold was a woman he had wanted in his bed for years. Catherine Wagner. Hellcat Catherine Wagner.

"It's two points if it goes in," he said.

"It's four if you recycle it."

He tossed the paper into the wastebasket. It missed. Catherine made a face.

His secretary was hopping up and down behind her. "I'm terribly sorry, sir—"

"That's okay, Mary." He gazed into Catherine's stormy eyes, then finally rose from his chair. "What can I do for you, Catherine?"

She walked into the room, her strides confident. Tall and slim, she moved with a grace that took a man's breath . . . and left him wondering if she would move the same way beneath him. Her beige silk skirt and high heels emphasized already very sexy legs, while her pale orange blouse was open to the breastbone. The lace edge of her modest chemise teased his senses with what was hidden, rather than what was exposed. Her shoulder-length hair was almost auburn in color and thick, enticing a man to touch the strands and see if they would wrap around his fingers like silken threads. Her features were fragile looking at first glance. At the second, one saw the set of her jaw. And at the third, the usually unfathomable expression of her eyes. The combination was always intriguing. But circumstances had always denied him a closer look. . . .

"Why is my grandfather's office locked?" she asked.

Miles gritted his teeth at the accusation underlying her tone. "Because it isn't in use," he answered. "You know that."

She bent down and picked up the wad of paper, but she didn't throw it in the basket. Instead she smoothed it out and refolded it, then tucked it into a skirt pocket.

He grinned. "What else do you recycle in there?"

Her expression was stony—as usual. Once, he had made a mistake with her. Only once. He'd been paying for it ever since.

"Ah, there you are, young man."

His grandmother swept into the room with a swirl of soft skirts and Chanel perfume. Lettice Kitteridge was silver haired and nearly eighty—and nowhere near ready for the rocker on the porch.

"I cannot believe," she exclaimed, "that you train your security people to deny your own grandmother the right to see you. They made me show identification before they would let me come up-stairs!"

Miles grinned and walked around his desk to kiss his grandmother's cheek. "It's a bank, Grand-mother. Not Disney World."

"And I'm a major stockholder!" she snapped.

"Then come more often, so they know you." He turned back to Catherine. Now that he was closer, the awareness already stirring his blood began to heat. He forced it away. "What did you need in your grandfather's office?"

"I need it opened. Please."

His eyes narrowed. Allan Wagner might have been her grandfather, but that didn't mean he would open a trustee's office for her. He had a responsibility as Philadelphia National Bank's executive director.

"Better show him some ID, Catherine," Lettice said. "This place is worse than Heathrow Airport! You're such a prig, Miles."

Miles snorted. Still, Lettice had a point. As a relative, Catherine did have some right to personal items. He was behaving like an overprotective jerk. Allan had been his friend, and he owed him more than this. There was still a slight problem with her request, however.

He began to explain. "There isn't anything—"

Catherine interrupted. "Are you refusing to open the office?"

"Well, no." He began again. "There's a—"

"Just open it, please."

He gave up. "If it makes you happy."

"It does."

"Fine." He went back around his desk and opened the middle drawer, taking out a set of keys.

He slipped his suit jacket from the valet and put it on, not bothering to button it. Catherine turned and walked out of the office. Miles followed more slowly with his grandmother. He grinned as he studied the tantalizing stretch of fabric across her thighs and derriere. If ever there was something to go to war over, it was Catherine's tush.

He'd follow like a lamb to the slaughter.

Catherine slowly let out her breath as she walked down the hall ahead of Miles and Lettice. She'd gone in like a lion, and she had gotten what she wanted. Maybe there was something to a "power" attitude. Her stomach was still flipping after facing down Miles Kitteridge, though. Few did it successfully, she knew. The man could have given Michael Douglas a run for the Gordon Gecko part in *Wall Street.*

She refused to admit that her blood was pumping hot through her veins for any reason other than a confrontation with the enemy. Miles Kitteridge might have a lean, hard body under his conservative three-piece suit, and he might have a face that was as lean and hard and attractive as the rest of him, but they weren't a consideration here. Neither were his blue-green eyes that seemed to probe beyond the surface, seeking all of her secrets.

She forced herself to take another deep breath as they reached her late grandfather's old office. Okay, so Miles was sexy as hell, but she knew what he was really like. A man with no integrity. She'd witnessed that one firsthand. She needed to remember, too, that he was "The Banker" for Wagner

Oil, and in thick as thieves with her greedy relatives.

She had to concentrate on why she was there at Philadelphia National—to find that codicil to her grandfather's will. Without it, the will would stand as read. With it, she could stop the madness. She had seen what an oil spill could do, and the sight had been sickening. Her grandfather had seen as well, and it had forever changed him. Changed them both. He had wanted the Utah land that Wagner Oil owned turned into a nature preserve. If he had put the land in a trust fund, it would have been protected. Now, unless she found that damn codicil, her family intended to ruin it in the name of Wagner Oil. She knew the codicil existed; Lettice had actually seen it. And the family members knew her grandfather had wanted to preserve the land. That didn't quite fit in with their strip-mining plans, however. Even her own parents . . .

Her grandfather's lawyers didn't have the codicil. She had also searched her grandfather's house and his office at Wagner with no success. He had been on the board of trustees for Philadelphia National, and this office was her last hope. Lettice would know it at a glance; that was why she was with her. Catherine smiled. Wouldn't Miles be surprised to know whose side his grandmother was really on?

Miles walked up beside her to unlock the door. She forgot everything at his closeness. Watching his hands in fascination as they smoothly turned the door handle, she wondered if they would be so expert on her body. The clean scent of cologne and male filled her nostrils. His profile was sharply defined, and she was intrigued by the faint lines around his eyes, those incredible aquamarine eyes. She knew he was five years older than her twenty-nine. He had been away to college when she was a teenager, then she had gone to college herself by the time he came home. When she returned after graduation, he had been married, and she had been engaged when he got divorced. They'd never had a chance for more than a kiss. . . .

Abruptly she felt the urge to reach out and touch his face, to feel his mouth on hers, to—

Catherine caught herself at the thought. Lord help her if she was really that desperate for a man that she would consider Miles Kitteridge. It aggravated her to know that he could bring out this kind of reaction in her, after what he had done to her three years ago. Why was it that men like him always appealed to women who should know better? It must be the reformer in the female sex, she decided wryly. Women were loaded with it.

He swung the door open and motioned for her to go in first. He had a funny kind of smile on his face that she couldn't read.

As she edged past him, he gazed down at her. Every muscle in her body tensed. She had the overwhelming urge to run her hand down the lapel of his gray suit and absorb the feel of soft wool and hard muscle. Ringing through her head was the litany, *I'm not engaged any longer . . . any longer . . .*

This wasn't good.

Catherine scooted into the office. She strangled on her sigh of relief when she caught sight of the room.

The bookshelves, the credenzas, the walls, and

the tables were empty. Not a single personal item, book, binder, or picture was visible. Even the top of the cherrywood desk was devoid of a telephone. Her grandfather had been wiped clean.

She strode over to the desk and yanked open one drawer. It was empty, except for a pack of Red Hots. No papers, no files, no nothing. That only confirmed her fears.

Fury shot through her, and she whirled around to face Miles. "What the hell have you done?"

"I haven't done a damn thing anyone else wouldn't have done," he snapped.

"Miles, honestly," Lettice said. "Can't you see this was a rude shock for Catherine?" She waved her arm around the empty room.

He frowned at his grandmother. "I tried to tell her, and you, that Allan's office was empty. Next time I'll be Avis and try harder, okay?"

Catherine sat down heavily in the leather swivel chair, its tall padded back and winged sides cushioning her in a dark cocoon. So much for a power attitude, she thought, when one didn't even bother to listen. He was laughing at her now. All the papers, everything, were already back in one of her relatives' hands. Now she'd never be able to ensure her grandfather's last wishes were carried out. Why couldn't he have given the codicil to her in the first place for safekeeping?

"Who did you send everything to?" she asked dully.

"Nobody," Miles said.

She bolted upright, completely astonished. "Nobody?"

He shook his head. "I asked your uncle Byrne what he wanted me to do with Allan's personal things, and he just shrugged at the time. You know the office here was more of a courtesy. Allan wasn't very active at the bank. I had my secretary file the bank things and pack up the rest."

She smiled happily. "I like you, Miles. You're smart, you're bright, you're very efficient. So where are the boxed-up things? In the bank basement?"

His eyebrows rose at her change of tone. "At my house."

Catherine swallowed. His house? She was positive the codicil had been stored here in the office. Where else could it have been? And now Miles had everything at his house. The question was: Did he know what he had? The answer had to be yes.

He was grinning at her. "You can come over this evening and get them if you like."

She blinked. Maybe, just maybe, he didn't know. She would have to change some major plans for the night if she was to go to his house. And she would have to be nice to Miles. She could do that.

"What time?" she asked.

"Eight. Come for dinner."

"Wonderful!" she exclaimed.

Looking at his charming smile and enticing body, she knew being nice was very dangerous. She'd been playing a dangerous game for a while, though. Surely she could handle this one.

"Lettice, of course you'll come too," she added, deciding not to be stupid. Besides, she would need the older woman's help.

"I thought you'd never ask," Lettice replied, smiling slyly.

Catherine smiled back. Her amusement faded

when she saw Miles's narrowed eyes. A shiver of premonition ran down her spine.

She had a feeling she would pay for this—in ways she hadn't imagined.

Dinner wasn't what she'd thought it would be. It was worse.

Catherine had been braced for an intimate meal. To her own disgust, she had gone through her closet like a madwoman, tossing clothes everywhere and satisfied with none. She'd finally settled on a pale yellow sheath as the best of the worst. Her hair and makeup had gone through several retakes, until she realized exactly what she was doing. Getting pretty for Miles. It didn't help to know it. And it had been especially deflating when she arrived at his house, only to discover he'd invited several other people, all business associates, including a lawyer whose wife kept giving Miles intimate smiles. The husband didn't seem to notice, or else he didn't care.

Catherine noticed. At each provocative look Mrs. Costmeyer sent Miles, an odd flash of jealousy swept through her.

Miles's response to the woman was distant but polite, yet Catherine couldn't tell whether he was uninterested or just putting up a front. Had he smiled intimately back when she wasn't looking? Probably. Still, she would have thought she'd catch him at it at least once.

If she were honest, she couldn't blame Mrs. Costmeyer for flirting with him. He looked terrific in his black sweater and trousers. The color was normally more suited to Nordic types, but it only enhanced Miles's dark looks.

Finally, dessert was served. Catherine took a couple of bites of the strawberry pie, drank her coffee, then patted her mouth with the linen napkin. She wanted nothing more than to get those boxes and get out fast. She'd love to kick Miles for not telling her about his other guests. All that anxiety for nothing. Maybe she'd kick him anyway. She couldn't believe she'd changed some very important plans for this.

"Did you say something, dear?" Lettice asked, taking her sweet old time with her slice of pie.

"No," Catherine said, smiling brightly. "Just enjoying the pie."

Lettice's gaze shifted to the Costmeyer woman, then back to Catherine in a meaningful expression. Catherine wished she knew what it meant. Maybe Lettice wanted the two of them to take the woman out and shoot her. Catherine smiled. It sounded lovely. And it would liven up dinner considerably.

Miles finished his pie and set down his napkin. "Please excuse Catherine and me for a few minutes. We have some business that can't wait any longer. Grandmother, will you play host for me?"

"Certainly," Lettice replied. She turned to one of the guests. "John, how is the market today?"

John Harland launched into what looked to be a long, detailed monologue. Lettice sat back in her chair, clearly settling in for the duration. Catherine rose, grateful to escape. Wall Street had already been dissected twice that night, along with the Hong Kong, London, and Toyko markets. As they left the room, she tried to ignore Miles's hand at the small of her back.

"I was ready to dig a tunnel out of there," he said after closing the door behind them.

"Why didn't you tell me you were having guests?" she asked, stepping away from him. "I didn't have to come to dinner. I could have just picked up Grandfather's things."

"Truthfully, I forgot about this. It's a pay-back business dinner." He shrugged. "One of those things where you owe a business associate a meal, even though there's no business to discuss. I hate them, and I'm very grateful I had you to rescue me."

"I understand completely," she said in a dry tone, thinking of the smiling woman back in the dining room. "Still, I suppose I shouldn't keep you. Which way to my grandfather's things?"

He turned left. "I put them in the garage."

He led her through the kitchen, past the catering people, and on into the attached garage. He turned on the light switch, revealing his cars.

Gas guzzlers, Catherine thought disdainfully as she passed a Corvette, a Mercedes, and a BMW. She had given up her own "Beemer" for a nice little two-door compact that got great mileage.

Several boxes sat on a shelf. Miles hoisted one down and set it on the hood of the BMW. Catherine had originally thought just to put them in her car and go home before opening them. Now she couldn't resist. She whipped open the tucked-in flaps.

The first thing that stared up at her was a picture of her and her grandfather taken when she was twelve.

"Oh," she said, swallowing back a rush of emotions. "Oh."

At the sound of her voice, Miles turned around from getting another box. She was gazing at something inside the carton, and to his horror, a single tear rolled off her cheek.

"Catherine." He put his arm around her in awkward comfort, not quite knowing what else to do. She sniffled. He got out his handkerchief and put it over her nose.

"Blow," he ordered.

"You blow." She pushed the handkerchief away, then swiped at her tears. "Really, Miles, it was just a sniffle. You didn't have to shove the handkerchief in my face." She paused. "You're being kind, and I'm snapping. I'm sorry."

"I understand. Allan was my friend too."

She smiled slightly, and he sensed she was softening to him a little. That pleased him. He was all too aware of her body close to his. It was as if the air pressure between them changed with each subtle shift and movement. Perfume swirled through his senses, mesmerizing him.

The strong urge to claim her, coupled with an overwhelming need to protect, surged through him. How Catherine provoked that response in him, he didn't know. He only knew that she did.

"I'm okay now," she said, and her firm voice shored up his faltering control.

Reluctantly, he let his arm drop and stepped away. Her armor might be back in place, but that didn't stop what he was feeling. He stared at her in frustration, wondering if she'd ever stop punishing him.

"I only asked you once to go to bed with me," he muttered.

She stiffened, not looking at him. "My wedding was three weeks away at the time," she replied in a cold voice.

He grabbed the second box and slammed it onto the hood of the car. "You weren't married yet."

"That didn't mean I was fair game." She yanked things out of the first box and slapped them onto the hood, half hoping she'd scratch the umblemished paint. "I had a commitment I wasn't about to break."

"It was dead in the water before it even got started. Anyone could see that."

Catherine gave him a glare worthy of his grandmother. He realized he might have gone too far with that last remark.

"I never had any intention to be another notch on your belt," she said, then added, "Or should we look lower?"

"Be my guest."

"No thank you."

He leaned against the car. "What's the matter? Afraid to find out you're attracted to me?"

She steadily met his challenging gaze. "I am not attracted to you."

"Then let's test that theory, shall we?"

He straightened and pulled her to him, covering her mouth with his before she could protest. He pried her lips open and thrust his tongue inside. At first she resisted as he searched the sweet interior, then her tongue mated with his in a way that sent his mind spinning. The soft wanting of her mouth rocked him. His blood pumped hot and heavy, surging like an unstoppable tidal wave. Her body fitted perfectly to his, her breasts barely caressing his chest in a slow torture. His fingers tightened around her arms, bringing her closer. The kiss was fiery, filled with every long-suppressed fantasy about her . . .

She broke away abruptly. He blinked, then grinned.

"So much for your theory about attraction," he said.

"And I was just thinking that you've been without a woman too long to kiss so heavy-handed," she replied, turning back to the boxes.

He refused to be baited. "I don't know, Catherine. My tonsils could tell a few tales about that kiss."

Her cheeks pinkened, and she rummaged more diligently through the boxes.

"Cat got your tongue?" he asked. "I'd be happy to find it again."

"Why don't you go see your friend in there, the smiling chimpanzee in heat . . ." Her voice trailed away, and she began to claw frantically around the items in the boxes. "It's not here!"

"What's not here?" he asked, watching as she literally tossed things onto the BMW's hood.

"The codicil!" she exclaimed, then froze. "Never mind."

He stared at her. "Codicil? What codicil? What are you talking about, Catherine?"

Her jaw squared stubbornly, then she made a face and sighed. "My grandfather's codicil to his will."

"Allan had a codicil?"

"Yes."

"But why don't the lawyers have it? The will was read months ago."

She glared at him. "I know that, and I don't know why the lawyers don't have it. He must have put it aside or something, meaning to file it with his own people—"

"How do you even know there is one?" he asked dubiously.

"Because *your* grandmother's seen it," she said, smiling sweetly.

"Really?"

"Yes, really. My grandfather had a huge parcel of land in Utah he wanted preserved. He didn't put it into trust. If I don't find the codicil, it will be strip-mined."

"Yes, I know," Miles said, remembering the original plans from several years ago. "But Allan wanted that—"

"No, he didn't," Catherine said vehemently. "The family knows he wanted that land to become a preserve, but they refuse to do it because it wasn't specified in the will. Wagner Oil wiped out an entire species of sea turtles in that Gulf of Mexico oil spill. Remember the headlines? Not to mention what it did to hundreds of miles of breeding beds and beaches. The destruction changed my grandfather. He never wanted to see such a thing happen again."

"I remember the spill very well," Miles said. "Allan insisted Wagner Oil pay for the entire cleanup. It cost the corporation tens of millions of dollars that year."

She suddenly went very still, and he frowned at the abrupt chill in the air. "Catherine?"

"Thank you for reminding me, Miles. I had

forgotten." She picked up the framed picture of her and her grandfather. "I'd forgotten a lot of things. And thank you for the dinner. It was delicious."

She walked out of the garage.

Catherine watched for the slightest movement to indicate the guards making their rounds. They shouldn't be, but her heart pounded fiercely with every passing second, and her fingers tightened around the bedsheets in a death grip.

She had decided not to do this that night . . . until Miles had reminded her of who and what she really was. Damn him, she thought. He had given her a kiss that shook her to her toes, then he'd calmly talked about millions of dollars in losses. She had thought for one moment of kindness that he had changed. Now she knew better. Miles Kitteridge would always care about the almighty dollar before anything else. He certainly hadn't cared about a commitment she'd made to another man. He'd thought it a joke then, and he thought it now.

No integrity.

But she would never forget that night. It had turned her life into a shambles. At the time, she'd been engaged to a man she'd met at law school. After graduation they decided to open a legal aid office for the disadvantaged. Of course, they'd need her money to finance it, but it would be a partnership. He passed the bar exam the first time, but she flunked twice. The next exam was just three weeks before the wedding. The pressure had been tremendous, and not wanting to overstudy the night before the exam, she went to a friend's party.

Miles had cornered her there. He had touched her hair, her cheek, her shoulder, keeping only a scant inch of air between them in a way that enticed her unbearably. Perhaps she'd always had a bit of a crush on him, and for a few minutes she'd enjoyed the idea that he was attracted to her too. And then he'd lightly kissed her and suggested they leave together. The worst part was, she had wanted to desperately. Somehow she'd resisted, somehow she had gotten away, though not with any finesse.

He had thrown her so completely, she'd gone into the bar exam with him looming in her mind, breaking her concentration. She'd had the worst score recorded in twenty years of testing. Her fiancé had called off the wedding, not wanting to be a "kept man," even until the next test. The man had been obnoxiously noble.

Miles had ruined her nice, neatly planned life. She hadn't bothered to try to pass the bar again, but had accepted her grandfather's offer to work in the research and development department at Wagner Oil. A year ago she'd been granted a seat on the board of directors. And that had been when she really began taking charge of her life again. At last she had a cause worth fighting for. If only she could find that damn codicil.

She wished she'd never said a word about it to Miles. She had a pretty good idea that if he found it, it would stay hidden.

She shook off the distressing thought. If her family wouldn't honor the codicil on their own, she'd just have to help them along. Tonight was the first in a series of missions to do just that.

And she'd better get started before she chickened out.

Finally satisfied that no guards were checking this area of the Wagner Oil refinery plant, she crept out of her hiding place, keeping to the dark shadows as much as possible. There weren't many. Floodlights illuminated nearly every cranny of the plant inside the fence and at least two hundred feet on the outside. Cars zoomed noisily above her on the Route 95 freeway. Even at five in the morning, the road sounded busy. She just hoped nobody noticed her for the next few minutes.

Taking a last deep breath and clutching one sheet to her, she raced across the open lighted space to the eight-foot-high fence. The barbed wire surrounding the top was not a deterrent. It was a help. She clambered up the fence as best she could and hooked one end of the sheet to the barbs, then leaped down and climbed up to hook the other end. The sheet unfurled in all its glory.

She raced back to her hiding spot and grabbed another sheet. After checking the grounds again, she repeated the process until there were four sheets lined up on the fence, their declarations visible to every car on the freeway.

Catherine breathed a sigh of relief when she reached her car and slipped inside. She started the little Sunbird and took off. When she was safe on one of the back streets of South Philadelphia, she grinned.

Earth Angel had struck. And right on time for rush hour.

Two

"Dammit! Who the hell is this Earth Angel?"

Byrne Wagner pounded his meaty hands on the wood table in Wagner Corporation's conference room to emphasize his question. Miles winced at the heavy blows, surprised Byrne hadn't marred the finish.

Catherine, who was seated across the table from Miles, shrugged. "Who knows? The press is clamoring for an answer to those signs, Uncle Byrne. Ted Koppel's called twice."

Out of all the Wagner directors called in for the emergency meeting, Miles thought, only she was calm. The rest were red faced with anger and nearly sweating with anxiety.

Byrne's face turned even darker. "We're not answering the press on a nut who hangs a bunch of bedsheets on our refinery plant's fence!"

Catherine smiled sweetly. "Can I quote you on that when I tell them 'No comment'?"

"You won't say a damn word, girl!"

Her smile never faltered. "I suggest somebody

say something. Otherwise we'll be accused of stonewalling in every major city newspaper."

"Catherine's right," Miles said. She stared at him, her eyes wide. He grinned, enjoying her astonishment at his agreeing with her. "That sign was pretty specific in its accusation," he went on, looking around the conference table. "The swifter and smoother our response, the less credence we'll give to the Earth Angel, whoever the nut actually is."

His gaze returned to Catherine. He admired her cool response to the crisis, even as he admired the way her wraparound blouse draped across her perfect breasts. How he would love to undo those buttons at the waist slowly and sensually, allowing the material to fall open . . . or feel it rip apart under his hands in a frenzy of lust.

That was the problem with Catherine, he thought. Both scenarios appealed mightily. Unfortunately, this wasn't the time for it. Besides, she'd been upset with him last night and he wasn't certain why. Was it that kiss? He could still taste the sweetness of her mouth, unique and made for him. He had a feeling that that was only part of her anger, though. At least this Earth Angel business gave him an opportunity to find out.

Miles grimaced at the thought of that environmental crazy. He had been dragged out of bed at six that morning by a frantic phone call from Byrne, insisting he attend this emergency meeting. By virtue of Philadelphia National's financial entanglements with Wagner Oil, he had a seat on the board of directors. Sometime during the night, Byrne told him, someone had hung a homemade sign on their fence. A very big sign that declared to every car on 95: WARNING! WAGNER OIL IS KILLING YOU BY DUMPING TOXIC WASTES INTO YOUR DRINKING WATER. STOP BUYING WAGNER OIL AND STOP KILLING YOURSELF TODAY!

Byrne was in a panic, and so was everyone else. Miles had to admit it wasn't the best way to start a morning. Nut or not, if this wasn't handled exactly right, it could explode in Wagner's corporate face.

"I don't see why we have to answer this outrageous allegation," Byrne said stubbornly.

"Because this company is responsible for the worst oil spill the world has ever seen," Catherine said.

"That just makes us an easy target," her father, Gerald, replied. "It's a ridiculous accusation, Catherine. I just saw a report on TV that the Delaware River is healthier than it's ever been. So how can we be polluting it?"

Miles raised his eyebrows at Gerald's lack of support for his own daughter. Catherine wasn't just the cool one, she was the only one making sense. The corporation needed to respond.

The door burst open, and one of the vice presidents rushed in. "The EPA just called! It's going to test the Delaware and Schukyll rivers around the plant for violations!"

Everyone groaned.

"Is there any truth to the accusation?" Sylvia asked. She was Byrne and Gerald's younger sister.

Byrne took a swig out of the antacid bottle by his side, then said, "Of course not!"

"We better hope not," Catherine said. "Has anybody checked this morning to make sure we're not leaking crude or by-products?"

Dead silence answered her.

"Have we checked any morning in recent history?" she asked in the driest of tones.

"Well . . . of course we check the system," Byrne sputtered.

Miles got a bad feeling as he watched the man glower like a frustrated bull about to charge. It was the same kind of feeling he always had right before the dollar took a nosedive on the foreign exchanges. It wasn't hard to see why. Allan's response to the oil spill had been swift and responsible, and because of that, the company hadn't lost credibility with the public. Sure, it had lost money on the cleanup, but they'd regained the profit structure, and more, the next year. Byrne was about to bungle this one, though.

"We must begin more stringent measures," Catherine said. "We need to turn the fleet toward double-hulled ships, stop strip-mining, explore other energy resources—"

Everyone groaned again. Miles had a vision of loans and more loans to finance the projects. Loans with *big* interest rates. Catherine was not only stunning, she was a banker's dream.

"This company had better take a reality check," she said, rising to her feet. "If there's twenty years left of fossil fuels, we'll be damn lucky."

Voices shouted her down.

"We're not here to talk about the future," Byrne said. "We're here to talk about how we're *not* going to respond to some nut. All in favor?"

"Now, wait a minute," Miles exclaimed, realizing Byrne was ramming a vote through.

"Aye!" most of the family called in loud, adamant voices.

"No!" Catherine snapped, her eyes blazing with anger.

She walked out.

Miles watched her go, her slim skirt tight against her hips and thighs. Nobody made an exit better than Catherine.

Catherine shut her office door and finally allowed herself to chuckle.

She'd never enjoyed herself more at a Wagner board meeting, although she had gotten angry at the end. She'd had this argument with them in the past, so their response wasn't new. Neither was hers.

Earth Angel had certainly stirred them into a frenzy, though. That was a sight to behold, and well worth the risk of putting up that sign. Her uncle had been spitting nails. And well he should, she thought. He knew they were "leaking" toxic by-products into the Delaware, because they did it from midnight to two A.M. every night. The plant manager had been suspiciously absent from the meeting this morning, and she wished she hadn't lost her temper before she'd been able to ask where he was. She would have loved to hear her uncle's answer.

She sat down at her desk, empty as usual, thanks to her uncle. The less the board members knew, the better, was his theory. Most of them liked it that way too. At least Earth Angel had gotten one of them thinking. Bless Aunt Sylvia for questioning her brother. Catherine wondered if she might actually get her aunt's support in the future. That would be a major miracle.

Reluctantly she acknowledged she had support already from a very unexpected source. She'd nearly fallen out of her chair when Miles had backed her up about the press. Why had he done it? He never did anything unless he had something to gain, so what did he expect to gain?

She didn't know, and that worried her. Miles worried her in more ways than she cared to admit. Only by sheer willpower had she kept her composure while sitting across from him. She could still taste last night's kiss, still feel the desire that had surged through her. Her gaze had kept wandering to him during the meeting, and she had to admit he looked good enough to make the cover of *GQ*.

Despite the argument swirling around, she'd been obsessed with wondering whether he wore a T-shirt under his white silk shirt. There had been a dark shadow on his chest, barely discernible but there. She had wanted desperately to unbutton the shirt and discover whether he had hair on his chest or not. Would it be silky or curly? She would have to run her palms across his flesh to find out . . .

She pushed away the dangerous thought. Miles's support of her meant nothing. He simply knew it was more advantageous to talk to the press than avoid them. He wasn't stupid.

Her office door swung open with a bang, and Miles himself strolled in like he owned the place. Her jaw dropped in astonishment.

"Since you barged into my office," he said, grinning at her, "I felt it only fair to return the favor."

"There isn't any secretary here to try to stop you," she commented, regaining her composure.

"True." He shut the door behind him. "Why don't you have one?"

"I don't rate."

His eyebrows arched. "What do you mean, you don't rate?"

Catherine took a deep breath. "My work load with research and development has been drastically reduced to twiddling my thumbs all day. It's tough for a secretary to take dictation on that."

"I see." He paused. "You know, if you hadn't gone off on a tangent, you might have persuaded enough of the board to your side."

"Is this Corporate Strategy 101?" she asked.

"You need the lessons." He sat down in the cast-off barrel chair in front of her desk, then glanced around. "Nice office."

She grimaced. "It's a dump."

He stared at her, his gaze seeming to probe through her. She tried to keep her own gaze from wandering. Whatever was under his shirt didn't matter to her. But looking straight into his eyes was sending shock waves along her nerve endings. The feel of his mouth on hers haunted her. She blessed the desk that separated them. It was an effective barrier—enough to allow her some semblance of control over her whirling emotions.

She forced herself to speak. "Why are you here, Miles?"

"Because I want some straight answers about the EPA testing. Is there something to worry about?"

She tilted her head. "Why do you ask?"

"Because Byrne is drinking Maalox like it's Perrier. I think there is something to worry about, and I think we're all going to look like a horse's backside because he's stonewalling the media instead of giving them a direct answer."

"Then we're going to look like a horse's backside," she agreed. She glanced at his shirtfront, but still couldn't tell what was underneath. Maybe he wore a Bart Simpson T-shirt. It tickled her to think that possibly emblazoned on Miles Kitteridge's chest was the legend, "Underachiever and proud of it."

"Why is there a paper bag by your desk?" he asked abruptly.

She glanced at the grocery sack she used to recycle her wastepaper. "My version of paper basketball."

"It's empty."

"I'm a lousy shot."

"I see." He paused, then dropped a major bomb. "Who do you think this Earth Angel is?"

She never moved. Somehow, she wasn't surprised at the question. But he didn't know, so she might as well enjoy herself. Smothering a grin, she shrugged casually. "Who knows? A nut, like you said."

"I've been thinking about that. I think it's someone who works here."

"Here?" Her voice squeaked.

He nodded. "Here at Wagner. Earth Angel might be a nut, but I have a feeling he or she is a knowledgeable nut."

Catherine waved her hand in dismissal. She'd better get him looking in another direction. "Personally, I think it's the Green Earthers," she said, naming the international environmental group. It was the truth in a way, since she was a member.

"They watch Wagner all the time. We've been a target of theirs for years."

"Maybe." He was silent for a moment. "I also came to apologize for last night. What did I do?"

A million things, she thought. And all of them to her body. "You did nothing. Why are you apologizing?"

"Because you walked out." He chuckled. "By the way, you did it with great discretion. I don't think my guests even knew you were angry."

"I wouldn't care if they did."

"I expect not. So are you going to give me a straight answer . . . or am I to assume the kiss was just too much for you?"

"I nearly swooned, Miles," she said, grabbing onto the banter. "I just couldn't be in the same room with you any longer. Otherwise I would have been shamelessly throwing myself at you. Happy now?"

"Thrilled to my toes." He continued gazing at her, clearly waiting for the real answer.

The real answer was that their values were poles apart, and that would always hinder any friendliness between them. She knew Miles would never understand why the almighty dollar didn't mean so much to her, and it wasn't worth the effort to tell him.

She shrugged instead. "My grandfather's things brought back a lot of memories. I was upset."

He smiled. "That wasn't it. You and Allan fought for years."

"Maybe I was regretting them," she said, scowling at him. "Not everyone is as coldhearted as you."

"Then why don't you try to warm me?"

She barely suppressed a gasp at the erotic images his words and husky voice inspired. He had ruined her life once, though. She was not about to be tempted into ruining it again. Besides, his heart was a lost cause.

"Thank you, but no." She rose from her chair. "I have to go, Miles, so could we end this now?"

He didn't move. "I noticed that you didn't bring up the missing codicil today. Why not?"

"Were you obsessed with the Twenty Questions game when you were a kid?" she asked, exasperated with him.

"No. Why?"

"Because you keep asking questions! And I didn't bring the codicil up because they know about it already. So why didn't you mention it, if you thought I was hiding it?"

"Because I didn't know if you were. Since it wasn't in Allan's bank things, what will you do? Oops, another question. I beg your pardon."

"Keep searching," she answered anyway. She rubbed her forehead, feeling the headache that had come with her lack of sleep growing fiercer. "Look, I'm sorry about the question thing. I really have to go, Miles. I have several appointments this morning . . ."

He rose from the chair. Finally. "And I still have a bank to run."

She hurried around her desk to the door, the headache almost vanishing in her eagerness to have him gone. As she passed him, he took her arm.

She stilled.

"I'd like to make up for dinner last night," he said.

She couldn't look at him. She was afraid to.

Every nerve in her body was screaming for her to look, while every shred of common sense was telling her no. The latter was winning out . . . so far.

But his hand was warm and firm on her arm, and his fingers held more strength than she'd expected. His body was only inches away. One slight movement on her part and she would be against him. The sharp clean scent of him surrounded her, spinning her senses into a cyclone.

"I'd also like to talk to you more about Allan's codicil," he went on. "And this morning's meeting. How about if I pick you up at eight?"

"Eight?" she repeated, her voice hoarse. Out of the corner of her eye, she caught sight of his shirtfront. Unable to resist, she tilted her head to get a better look.

"Nine?" he asked.

"For what?"

"Dinner. Just the two of us this time. I promise."

Mesmerized, she stared at his chest. The dark area was definitely no Bart Simpson T-shirt. But she still couldn't tell if the chest hair was silky like Alec Baldwin's, or curly like Tom Selleck's.

"Catherine, you haven't answered me."

"What?" she said, blinking. She looked up, and that was her mistake.

She was caught in a sensual gaze that stripped away every shred of hidden emotion. His mouth was a bare inch away. Awareness thundered through her. She knew it showed in her face, but she couldn't control her reaction.

Miles muttered her name and pulled her to him, his mouth capturing hers in a deep kiss. Her control shattered, and she opened to him, entwining her tongue with his. He let go of her arm and wrapped her in a tight embrace. Every inch of her was finally and satisfyingly against him. Her blood pulsed at the feel of his hard body. Desire long suppressed swirled inside her. She wound her arms around his shoulders, her fingers digging into his jacket.

His tongue teased and tortured her, easing away and surging back over and over again, until she was moaning helplessly. She tasted and teased and tortured him back in feminine repayment. Everything swept through her in seven different directions all at once. She knew no other man would ever tie her up and turn her inside out with one kiss the way Miles did.

Unconsciously, she smoothed her hand down his chest, groaning at the feel of silk and hard muscles. And chest hair. She had never been so fascinated with what was under a man's shirt before, and she was gratified it was everything her fantasy wanted it to be.

Miles finally lifted his head. He buried his face in her hair, his breath hot against her ear.

She moaned into his chest. Some corner of her mind was trying to warn her about something, but the waves of desire coursing through her washed the voice away.

"Catherine," he whispered, his hands caressing her back.

"Miles." His name was as sensuous as the rest of him.

"Catherine."

She shivered and rubbed her hands against his shirtfront. Silky all the way.

He stepped back from her.

Disoriented, she opened her eyes. He'd left her drained and wanting.

He smiled a knowing smile. "It's my turn to make a grand exit. I'll pick you up at eight."

He walked out of her office before she could blink.

As soon as the door shut behind him, everything came crashing down. Catherine cursed her shameful reaction to him . . . and his ego. Like hell, she'd meet him at eight that night.

Like hell.

Three

"Is there really a codicil?"

Miles watched his grandmother nibble on a paté sandwich before replying. He had taken her to afternoon tea at the elegant Barrymore Room atop the Bellevue for some answers to his growing questions. He had quite of few where Catherine was concerned.

Lettice finally set down the sandwich. "Do you know that your cousin Rick did not once take me to afternoon tea at the Ritz in London when I was there a few months ago? We went to Madame Toussaud's instead."

"Did you give him hell for being negligent?" Miles asked, amused by her aggrieved tone.

"Better than that," Lettice said. She smiled in satisfaction. "I married him off."

"And if I believe that, you've got a bridge to sell me, right?" Miles said, laughing. He'd heard family grumblings for a year or so about his grandmother meddling in his cousins' private lives. Naturally, she'd never get away with it with him. "Now what about this codicil of Allan's? I wanted to ask you last night, but you left shortly after Catherine did."

"That's what you get for that mess of a dinner, Miles."

"Grandmother," he prompted.

"Allan showed the codicil to me months ago." She sipped her tea. "He'd had it drawn up by a new lawyer. He said his own were in cahoots with Byrne."

"Can you remember who the lawyer was?"

She shook her head. "That name eludes me. Catherine's been after me to remember, and I've racked my brains with no luck. Are you going to help her find the codicil? She can save Wagner Oil with it."

"Knowing the family, they would contest it."

"You mean Byrne. But there's enough of them who wouldn't want the scandal. They would stop Byrne." She arched her eyebrows. "I see you already had one scandal this morning."

Miles grimaced. The media were having a field day with the company's "No comment." "Catherine couldn't get them to see reason. Neither could I."

Lettice poured more tea into her cup. "You like Catherine."

He grinned, remembering the kiss in her office . . . and the results. He still didn't know how he'd kept his control. "I'm taking her to dinner tonight."

"How surprising," Lettice murmured. "It'll make up for last night's fiasco."

He frowned. Something in his grandmother's expression bothered him. Did she know about the kiss in the garage? How could she? He couldn't see Catherine telling her.

"So where are you taking her?" Lettice asked.

"A very intimate restaurant." He smiled, antici-pation building inside him. This time, the evening would be perfect. He had seen to that. "She'll love it," he added.

"I am pleased."

It sounded like Lettice's seal of approval, Miles thought in amusement.

"You would hardly know Devlin is your twin," she murmured.

Miles shrugged. "Dev does as he pleases. So do I. What brought him up, anyway?"

"A thought." Lettice shrugged, then changed the subject. "You know, if you do help Catherine find the codicil, she would be grateful. *Very* grateful."

Miles steepled his fingers together. His grand-mother just might be on to something.

She was making the worst mistake in her life. Maybe.

Catherine gazed into the full-length mirror and grinned at her reflection. She knew she shouldn't be going out with Miles. But it was too prime an opportunity to resist, and she was glad she'd realized that. Miles was used to elegant women, so she had a pretty good idea what the date would be like.

She had just ensured he wouldn't get it.

In fact, she'd guaranteed that Miles would never ask her out again. Much better than not showing up in the first place, she decided, and mentally patted herself on the back for her shrewdness.

Still, Miles was the most dangerous man she'd ever encountered. He seemed to have a control over her body that she just couldn't shake. And if he found out about Earth Angel . . .

Catherine shuddered. Maybe this wasn't such a good idea, after all.

The doorbell to her Center City town house rang. A regiment of butterflies immediately invaded the pit of her stomach. She grabbed the hair spritzer and sprayed it on her hair, scrunching up the strands in a last-minute lift. The image in the mirror restored her confidence in handling Miles.

"What the heck," she said out loud. "You only live once, so it might as well be on the wild side. And I can't wait to see his face."

The door had no sooner opened than Miles felt all his breath whoosh out of his lungs.

Catherine was . . . not the Catherine he'd been expecting. She was dressed in a black leather mini and an off-the-shoulder blue knit top that clung to her torso. No bra, he thought as shock shot through him. The black patterned stockings and very high heels had his chest squeezing in an invisible vise. She's topped her outfit off with clunky bead jewelry and a hairdo that was artfully tangled in windblown fashion. He vaguely remembered hearing the term "big hair" somewhere. It certainly applied here. Her makeup was heavier than he'd ever seen before, and she'd done something to emphasize one eye.

The whole effect, rather than being displeasing, was extremely sexy. But this was all wrong for the evening he'd planned. La Fourchette was definitely out. She'd never get past the maitre d'. He made an immediate mental change of plans, not wanting to embarrass her.

"Miles, come in," she said, smiling.

"Thank you." From somewhere he managed to find enough air to speak. His heart was thumping painfully, and he dimly wondered if he was having a heart attack. He'd always had a feeling Catherine would kill him. "You look gorgeous."

For some reason annoyance flitted over her face. "I'll just get my jacket," she said, and turned toward the living room.

His feet automatically followed, as if he were under a spell. Before he knew it, he was in the middle of the room.

What the decor said about Catherine was an eye-opener. He'd been expecting . . . Actually, he didn't know what he'd been expecting. But to his delight, the room was tastefully furnished in 1920s art deco, with a Chinese carpet and gilt-trimmed *torchère* lamps. The furniture consisted of intricately inlaid wood veneer tables and tapestry-upholstered chairs. Movie posters hung from the walls, and he sensed they were originals.

"Ready," she said, breaking into his reverie.

Her black leather jacket matched her black leather skirt, and made him think she'd look right at home on the back of a motorcycle.

"Great," he said, without blinking. "Shall we go?"

"Where are we going?" she asked.

Good question, he thought. "It's a surprise."

It was a surprise all right, Catherine acknowledged, looking down at the steam table of gourmet fast food.

"The beef stir-fry is terrific," Miles said as he helped himself to spinach salad. "So's the home-made pasta."

Never would she have thought dinner would be at Eden's, a self-service restaurant. She should have known, though. He hadn't even faltered over her outfit. He actually thought she looked gorgeous. Wonderful. Somehow, he was still in control of the evening, and she had no idea what had gone wrong.

The glorified cafeteria was crowded with yuppies getting a meal before heading home or before going out for the evening. She had to admit that neither Miles, in his business suit, nor she looked out of place. He stayed by her side as they went through the line, just close enough to keep her awareness on edge.

"Do you know that Styrofoam plate your salad is on will be around for at least a hundred years?" she asked as they slid their trays along the counter.

"Do they keep reusing it?" he asked in return.

"No!" she exclaimed, astonished at his naiveté.

"Good. I couldn't imagine how they'd get the Italian dressing off. That stuff would eat through concrete. By the way, the Italian dressing is the pits."

She shook her head. "Miles, it doesn't biode-grade."

"I know it doesn't. I just said so."

"Not the dressing. The plate."

He looked down at it. "Oh."

"Come on," she said, moving ahead. Even if she was a bit disgruntled, the food smelled exotic and wonderful, and she was starving. "You're one heck of a date, Miles Kitteridge."

"Yes, I know," he said, laughter in his voice.

Later, she had to admit dinner was delicious. But the casual atmosphere of the restaurant made her relax with him. Miles surprised her by keeping the conversation light, not touching on business or what had happened that morning. They talked about their likes and dislikes, discovering they both preferred hamburgers with no cheese, swimming for exercise, and Harry Connick, Jr. They both had no understanding of art and hated sauces on anything. Miles claimed they were traitors to their sophisticated upbringing.

"Just because of those two things?" she asked, laughing.

"They're the foundation of every snooty school the world over," he replied. "They'd burn us at the stake for heresy, my friend."

"I still won't understand Picasso."

"It's a great investment, that's all I know."

"Philistine."

"That's me."

To her further surprise, he took her to a rowdy nightclub after the meal.

To her horror, everyone was dancing the lambada.

Spotlights swept over the crowd, the only illumination in the smoky room. And what they illuminated! Catherine swallowed as she watched couples gyrating wildly on the dance floor, while pressed so tightly together that a dime couldn't be squeezed between them.

"Could I have a drink?" she shouted to Miles

above the music that vibrated sensually deep in-side her.

He paused in shedding his suit jacket to give to the coat check. Clearly he was readying himself for action. "A drink?"

"Yes. Liquid in a glass, with ice cubes. A drink. I'm very thirsty." She waved her hand toward the cluster of booths, couches, and tables in the seat-ing area.

"If you like." He looked so disappointed, she smothered a giggle.

"Come on. Let's get a table before the music stops."

Not a single table was empty. Catherine began to panic until she spotted some space on the upper level, along a railing that overlooked the dance floor. She dragged Miles over, and they squeezed in together. People stared at them, then adjusted to make room. To her consternation, the women's gazes seemed to linger on Miles. He snagged a harried waitress, and they ordered drinks.

Catherine kept her back to the dance floor. She considered it necessary to her sanity. She was already shoulder-to-shoulder with Miles, and her nerve endings sizzled with awareness as his shirt-sleeve brushed her skin. The hardness of his arm was all too apparent under the silk. This was nearly as bad as the dancing.

"I'll bet the media is camped out on my uncle's doorstep," she said, deciding to bring the conver-sation around to the original purpose of the din-ner.

"As long as they're not on mine," he said, watch-ing the dancers below. He turned and grinned at her. "Or on yours."

She didn't like the sound of that. "He refuses to listen to reason."

Miles leaned sideways, his hip against the railing. Catherine gulped in air. He was so damn close.

"Let's not talk about your uncle," he said in a low voice. He was almost touching her ear with his lips in order to be heard. She shivered at the sensation of his breath on her skin as he added, "Let's dance."

"I thought talking was the whole point of dinner," she managed to say coherently. "That's what you said this morning."

"I was a fool." He gazed down at her. His features were taut. She could feel him staring at her breasts and wished her top was just a little higher. "Dance with me."

Her face heated. Every part of her heated. "I . . . we ordered drinks, remember? She'll never find us if we're dancing."

He cursed and leaned back against the rail again.

Catherine found she could breathe once more. She had a feeling it would be a real tug-of-war to stay off the dance floor.

"So tell me exactly what is going on at Wagner," he said.

"You should know."

"But I don't."

She looked at him questioningly. He shrugged. "I'm not in on the day-to-day operations, you know that. I'm on the board as a courtesy, because of the bank's involvement. Allan had my proxy, and I had his for his bank trustee position. You should know how the system works by now. You were raised on this stuff, just as I was."

She frowned. She did know, but she'd also seen Miles at too many meetings recently to believe he was a silent director. Still, if he wanted to play innocent, she could oblige. "Byrne refuses to do anything that could reduce the profits of the corporation. All the jobs that have anything to do with expanding our safety procedures, he eliminates. He'd rather save a dime than follow EPA standards."

"Come on, Catherine," Miles said in a disparaging tone. "He's not that foolish."

She set her jaw to keep her temper under control. "I'm perfect proof, Miles. Under my grandfather my job with R & D was to monitor operations development for potential environmental problems. When my uncle became chairman of the board, my entire team was eliminated, and now I sit in my office with a figurehead title and absolutely nothing to do."

"Do you think someone from your team is the Earth Angel?"

Catherine choked. "I doubt it, I really do," she said, recovering quickly. "I told you, it's probably the Green Earth people. Everyone on my team is working for other companies, anyway, so no one's disgruntled."

He nodded at her logic. She suppressed a sigh of relief.

"I asked my grandmother about the codicil," he said. "She says there is one."

Anger boiled up inside her. She spun to face him. "Did you think I lied about it?"

"No." He paused. "Actually, I didn't think about you at all. I only wanted to confirm its existence."

His words only angered her more. "I am not a liar, Miles Kitteridge."

"I never said you were."

"You just said you had to confirm what I had said."

"That's not what I—" The waitress appeared at that moment. Miles straightened and grinned. "Ah, saved by the drinks." He handed her a tall glass. "Here, Catherine, drink up your Perrier and cool down."

She eyed him narrowly as she sipped her drink. It aggravated her to realize that he could press more buttons than she ever knew she had. Of all the people in the world, she just couldn't understand why it was he who provoked her on every level. She'd met men who were better looking, who had more charisma, and who were certainly more sensitive. But it was Miles who could drive her over the edge with one look, and cause her to lose her control with one word.

The only good thing at the moment was that she finally had her drink in her hand and he *couldn't* ask her to dance. She wondered how long she could spin this out without looking as if she were avoiding him.

"What went wrong with your marriage?" she asked, then nearly groaned aloud. Of all the things to dredge up in desperation!

He shrugged, apparently not offended. "Sometimes young men marry with their . . . They don't think before they marry."

"You're telling me you married for physical attraction?" she asked, feeling a sharp pain twist oddly through her middle.

"No, not really. It's just that you're feeling like

Mr. Macho Protector of this vulnerable young thing. It's not until afterward that you realize how *wearing* wearing that mantle is."

"So you dumped her because she was a sweet young thing, and you wanted someone brighter."

He gazed at her, his eyes reminding her of cold ice. "Catherine, you are like talking to the razor's edge sometimes."

"I was only clarifying your words for my mind," she said, smiling sweetly. In a way, this verbal sparring was just as exciting as kissing him.

"That wasn't what I meant, and you damn well know it," he snapped, turning back to the crowd below.

Good, she thought. He was angry with her. That meant no dancing. Desperation had its hidden good points.

"So why didn't you marry Mr. Wonderful?" he asked after knocking back his drink.

"Because he dumped me," she said without thinking.

He turned back, his eyebrows raised. "He dumped *you*?"

She glared at him, angry with him for playing dumb and angry with herself for not taking more care with her answer. "Come on, Miles. You know all about it. Everyone does."

"All I know is the wedding never came off. You wouldn't return any of my calls at the time."

"There were only two." His lack of interest had irrationally angered her then, just as remembering it did now. "Besides, I had no intention—"

"—of being a notch on my belt," he finished for her. He lifted his glass in a salute. "I got the message at the time. So what did happen?"

"I flunked the bar for the third time," she said, shrugging in her turn. "We were supposed to go into partnership after the wedding. I had the . . . financing. When I couldn't be a true partner, Robert didn't want to be a 'kept' man, so he called off the marriage."

A part of her couldn't believe she was calmly telling this to the man who had caused that particular disaster in her life. But the last thing she wanted Miles to know was how strongly he affected her. It would feed his ego to learn she had been so thrown by his callous invitation.

"I never knew you were going to be a lawyer," he said.

She clenched her jaw. No "Gee, I'm sorry to hear that." No "He was a fool." Not one shred of sympathy. Why should she have expected any from a man who had no integrity? He had wreaked his havoc and gone on his merry way. "Yes, I went to law school. I even graduated."

He eyed her narrowly. "You're stropping that razor."

She took a deep breath to calm herself. She was not about to make a fool of herself again. "Let's just say I don't remember that time with joy and hallelujah."

"We're getting off the subject at hand," he said. "And the subject at hand is 'Let's dance.'"

"No," she said, trying not to panic. "We're supposed to be talking about Wagner Oil and my grandfather's codicil."

"That's only what you think." He stopped another waitress, then took Catherine's glass out of her hand and set it on the woman's tray. His own joined hers.

"But I wasn't finished," Catherine said, watching his movements in doomed fascination.

"Now you are."

Taking her elbow, he escorted her to the dance floor. Catherine went on leaden feet, knowing that to refuse would seem childish. Her brain scrambled for a reasonable excuse. None came to mind.

"Help me, Lord," she muttered.

"What?" he asked, bending low. "I didn't hear you."

"Miles, I don't think—"

As they neared the floor, the music changed from the frenetic beat of drums and guitars to a soft ballad. A plain old slow dance. Catherine smiled brilliantly and stopped a few vital steps from the dance floor. "Music's changed. Well, that's tha—"

"No, it's not." He spun her into his arms and walked her right onto the floor. "We'll just have to dance like this."

She was helpless to do anything else. Her body was breast to chest and hip to hip with his. His hand was at the small of her back, his fingers pressing her into him. Their thighs brushed together, his slipping lightly between hers. He kept her one hand wrapped in his, tucked into his chest. Her left hand rested lightly on his shoulder, and it took all the effort she had not to explore the hard muscles under the silk shirt.

The music faded; the other dancers were barely on the edge of her consciousness. Every inch of her torso was aware of every inch of his. Every sense was aware of his breath against her hair . . . his scent imprinting on her brainwaves . . . his mouth just there for the tasting . . .

She had been terrified to dance the blatant lambada with him, but this was much worse. The lambada was all sex and no tenderness. As they swayed to the gentle rhythm, she felt as if they were making love in front of everyone—slowly, prolonging the passion in a test of control before a wild burst of ecstasy erupted.

"You feel so right," he murmured. "I knew you would."

Some shred of sanity told her to keep it light. "I bet you say that to all the girls."

He lifted his head and stared into her eyes. The sweeping lights hid his expression. "Hardly."

She laughed, and it sounded like a donkey caught in quicksand. That was about how she felt. "You give a very impressive business dinner, Miles."

He looked down between them, obviously admiring the swells of her breasts crushed against his chest. "You are a very impressive business dinner partner."

The heat of embarrassment flooded her face as a deeper, more volatile heat flooded her abdomen. At this rate, she would be in his bed before midnight.

"I think I'm going to be sick," she groaned, appalled at her uncontrollable reaction to him.

Miles immediately stopped dancing and stepped away from her, his hands tight on her upper arms. He peered at her intently. "You're going to be sick?"

She realized he'd overheard her and actually thought she was unwell. She seized on the notion.

"Yes," she said, slumping and letting his hands take more of her weight. "The smoke . . . my stomach . . ."

"Right. We'll get you home." He hustled her off the dance floor and toward the exit.

Catherine went along quietly. Hell's bells, she thought in awe. She'd just performed a miracle.

They arrived at her place in record time. There was one little hitch at the door.

"I'll stay awhile to make sure you're okay," Miles said.

The gentlemanly gesture really did set her stomach to churning. "I appreciate the offer, but I'll be fine with a little rest. All that smoke just got to me. Like I told you in the car, my allergy to it flares up from time to time."

"I don't know." He frowned at her, peering at her in a way Sherlock Holmes would have admired. "I have to admit you don't look as washed out as you did on the dance floor."

Thank goodness for stark lighting, she thought. She turned her various keys in the right locks and opened the door. "Just getting out of there helped. I'm really sorry about this."

He waved his hand. "Don't worry about it."

"Good night, Miles."

"Good night, Catherine." He stepped forward . . .

She quickly shut the door on him before he could kiss her. If he did, he'd discover how *un*sick she really was. She pressed her ear to the hard wood until she heard his footsteps fade from the stoop, then she leaned back and sighed in relief. It had been a narrow escape. And one she would never repeat.

Next time she would risk looking stupid and silly rather than go out on another "business" dinner with Miles.

That decision made, she went off to bed.

• • •

Things didn't go quite as he'd expected, Miles mused, but the evening had turned out to be extremely profitable.

He tucked his arms under his pillow and stared at the ceiling. Sighing, he admitted his wasn't the bed he'd been hoping to wind up in. Despite that, he couldn't help feeling he'd made quite a bit of progress with Catherine that night. She had opened up to him, especially about her failed wedding.

He made a face at the thought of her disappearing fiancé. The stupid, self-righteous bastard. He would love to have the man in front of him right now for making such a mess in Catherine's life. Mike Tyson would be envious of the result. He'd always thought Catherine deserved better than her fiancé, but he never would have wished for her to be hurt like that. She must have been humiliated.

A wave of protectiveness rose in him, deeper and stronger than any he'd felt before. He wouldn't have expected to feel protective of Catherine. She didn't seem to need it. He wondered, though, just how much hurt she hid under her armor.

He sensed that despite her easiness with him during the evening, some barriers were nowhere near ready to come down. It would take a long time at this rate. Maybe his grandmother was on the right track about helping Catherine find the codicil. Miles grinned.

It would be interesting to see just how grateful Catherine would be.

•　　　•　　　•

Catherine carefully examined the sideview mirrors for any early morning traffic on the back road, then slowly drove the truck into the brush. The small dump truck made its own track through the wooded area, crushing bushes and underbrush under its large-tread tires. She silently begged forgiveness for the destruction, but knew the woods would cover her "road" within a week.

She had thought sleep would come easily that night, after her evening with Miles ended so precipitately. But she'd tossed and turned, Miles Kitteridge at every view. She decided in the early hours of the morning that if she couldn't sleep, she might as well get moving on Earth Angel's next assignment.

Damn that man, she thought. The whole evening had backfired on her. First she'd lost the controlling hand, then she'd nearly lost control of herself. If she hadn't uttered those mindless words . . .

Miles could hurt her badly and walk away without a backward glance. There was a calculating coldness under his charm. He was only interested in her because he had a second opportunity with her, and she had denied him once before.

He was up to something about Wagner Oil, she mused. Who did he think he was fooling with all those supposedly innocent questions? He was the banker. He *had* to know what her uncle was doing. She bet her salary he was in cahoots with Byrne.

She reached the creek before she expected to, and had to stand on the brakes when the bank came up in a rush.

The two-ton truck stopped with plenty of room to spare. Catherine got out and observed her objective. The creek narrowed nicely at the bend in front of her. She was about a half mile down from Wagner's Wissahickon paint subsidiary, outside Philadelphia. The previous week, the county had detected leakage farther down the creek, nearer the city. There were enough businesses and sewage treatment plants along the banks that they weren't able to trace the culprit before the toxins were diluted by the water.

Catherine smiled grimly. Earth Angel knew.

She climbed into the cab again, grateful that the dump truck, even fully loaded, was only slightly harder to handle than a pickup. She carefully backed it around, weaving in and out of the trees. Even more carefully, she brought the rear end of the truck nearly to the bank.

She got out of the cab and walked to the back of the truck, humming the "1812 Overture." When she reached the part where the cannons fired, she pressed a button.

The truck bed rose into the air, its load of clean dirt hanging precariously at a forty-five-degree angle. Rivulets dribbled off the earthen slope.

"Dadada-*de*-dadada-*de*-dada!" she sang out, and hit another button.

The dirt whoosed out of the dropping tailgate right on cue. It settled onto the narrow creek bed, effectively damming the water at the bend. The creek would eventually erode the earth . . . but not before the dam caught the runoff being leaked from a hidden pipe at the Wagner plant.

Catherine got a shovel out of the truck cab and walked into the knee-deep water. The newly created mud sucked at her rubber boots. Whistling, she began to spread the dirt around. To make it pretty. She reminded herself to call the EPA, the county, and the press after she got home. She also reminded herself to dispose of the boots. They wouldn't be fit for wearing after she was done.

She chuckled. It would be interesting to see how Miles reacted to Earth Angel's latest exploit.

She couldn't wait to find out.

Four

When Catherine was finally back in her town house, she sighed in relief. Being a pollution commando was heck on the nerves.

She glanced down at her boots. A thin rim of white gunk was drying around the ankles. Clearly her dam was working, as the paint by-products were already collecting at that point of the creek. Wrinkling her nose, she wondered how she was going to get the boots off without touching them. She wasn't about to move off the foyer mat to walk to the kitchen and get gloves. She'd ruin her carpet. But she wasn't about to touch the boots to take them off there.

"Great planning," she muttered, wishing she'd come through the garage.

Her doorbell rang. She froze, panic rushing through her. She couldn't have been traced already!

She forced herself to think logically. She had rented the truck at a gas station in the suburbs, and bought the dirt at a nursery in another suburb. No, they couldn't have found her out so quickly. Besides, nobody could possibly know about the dam yet.

The doorbell rang again, then someone pounded on the door, nearly shooting her off the mat.

"Catherine!" Miles bellowed.

All the logic swept out of her head.

The doorbell rang over and over, as if he were leaning on it. "Catherine, are you okay? Catherine, answer me! Catherine!"

She muttered a barnyard curse and wondered if she could get away with acting as if no one were home.

"Catherine!"

"What?" she screamed back reflexively, then soundly cursed again.

The doorbell ringing immediately ceased. The silence on the other side was almost as deafening. Finally, Miles asked, "Are you okay?"

"Yes, I'm okay," she called. In dread, she waited for the accusation and the demand to open the door so they could drag her away to prison forever.

Another, longer pause ensued. "I called earlier and there was no answer."

"I was . . . in the bathroom."

"Why?"

"Why do you think?" She looked heavenward in supplication.

"Oh. Can I come in?"

"What for?"

"To make sure you're all right."

"But I just told you I was okay."

"Catherine, I came to check on you because you were sick last night." She could hear the exasperation in his voice. "Now just let me in so I can see that you really are better."

"Oh." It finally sank in that he was there for a gentlemanly reason. She glanced down at the boots, the jeans, and the sweatshirt. One look, and he'd get the message. "It was lovely of you to come, Miles. I truly appreciate it. But I'm perfectly fine this morning. I told you last night I only needed to get out of the smoke and get some rest—"

"Then why won't you open the door?"

"Ah . . . I'm not dressed."

"I don't care. I just want to see that you're all right. You looked horrible last night. I never should have left you alone."

Of all the times to be a gentleman, she thought with irritation. "Miles, really—"

"Open the damn door, Catherine. I'm not leaving until you do."

He meant it. She panicked again. Now what? "Ah . . . well . . . just a minute."

She turned and raced through to the kitchen, whipped off the boots by the garage door, cursed that she'd forgotten to put on gloves, washed her hands, then tore up the stairs to her bedroom. She rolled up her jeans, threw on a neck-high velour robe, then ran back downstairs. She took a deep breath to calm herself, smiled wanly, and opened the door.

Miles barged inside.

Catherine glanced outside for the police, security guards, one big Doberman, anything that looked remotely like a bust. Her stoop was clear.

"I knew it!" Miles exclaimed, scrutinizing her.

"Knew what?" she squeaked.

"Look at you, all sweating and bundled up like that. I knew I should have stayed last night."

She swiped at her brow and was amazed to feel moisture on her skin. The heavy robe on top of her regular clothes wasn't helping, either. Still, it was better that he thought she was sick than to discover what she was really doing.

"It's just a touch of the flu," she began.

"Flu! I thought it was an allergy."

"Allergy. Flu." She waved her hand. "Sometimes they start out the same. You know how it is."

"Well, you should be in bed." He took her arm and moved her into the living room.

"I was in bed," she lied deftly, "until you tried to break down the door. Never do that to a single woman in the city. We get out our guns and blow people away for less."

"Do you have a gun?" he asked.

"No, don't be ridiculous. I just meant you scared me half to death." She dug in her heels as he whirled her around. "Where are we going?"

"You are going back to bed."

She turned, pulling him with her, and marched him back toward the door. "I will, as soon as you leave."

He pointed her toward the stairs again. "You get in bed first, and I'll bring you some tea."

She turned him back. "I'll get it when I'm ready."

"Catherine!"

"Miles!"

They glared at each other. Finally, Miles said, "Get in the bed, Catherine. I don't have time for this nonsense."

"Well, why didn't you say so? You've seen me, now just go—"

She squawked as he swept her up into his arms and strode toward the stairs. She scrambled to yank down the robe and keep the Chinese collar high around her throat.

"Miles, this is silly," she said primly. "Put me down and I promise to walk to my bedroom and then you can go back to your bank."

He grinned. "And miss this opportunity to show off my Galahad traits? Not on your life." His fingers shifted along her leg. "If I didn't know better, I'd swear you were wearing clothes under this robe."

"I . . . got the chills." She smiled at her adept answer. "I did put on something warmer than a gown."

His grin disappeared. "I should have stayed."

He negotiated the stairs easily. Catherine wanted to squirm out of his embrace, but knew she'd probably send them both tumbling down the steps. The fingers of his one hand were spread uncomfortably close to her breast, though, and her nostrils were filled with the scent of his cologne. That triggered something inside her. She tried to keep her gaze focused on the railing, but out of the corner of her eye she could discern his suit collar, his white shirt snowy against his jawline. His skin was tan and completely smooth, yet she could tell that by the afternoon, he'd have a shadow of a beard. Interesting, she thought, then wondered why she was so fascinated.

"Which room?" he asked, when they reached the top of the stairs. His voice was hoarse.

"In the front." Hers sounded no better.

The moment he stepped over the threshold, she felt the invasion. She was allowing him into the most private of rooms, no matter how innocent the reason. Now she did squirm, and he set her down.

Miles looked around at the floral draperies and white sheers, the striped wallpaper and cherry-wood bureau, the wide bed and its plump frilly comforter. One side was rumpled as if in invitation.

Catherine swallowed, wondering what the room told him about her. Probably more than she cared to have him know.

"Could I have that tea now?" she asked, desperate to get him out of there.

He turned and looked at her. She wilted under his sensual gaze.

"Sure," he said.

Without another word, he left the room.

"Yes, she's sicker than she's letting on . . . I know there are nurses for hire . . . No, I can't stay, Grandmother, I have a meeting at the bank . . . Well, why do you think I'm asking you?"

"I have no idea," Lettice said smartly. "I am not a nurse. If Catherine is that sick, then call in one or take her to the hospital."

Miles grit his teeth together and counted to ten. His grandmother was exasperating—as usual. Gripping Catherine's kitchen telephone tighter, he said, "She's not dying. She has the flu, and I need someone to watch over her, make sure she doesn't get out of bed, and fix her tea and things. I don't have time to arrange for a nurse, so can you come?"

"You surprise me, Miles," his grandmother said.

Her voice was faint as if she were murmuring to herself. Louder, she added, "Yes, I'll come."

"Great." He smiled in pleasure and hung up the telephone.

The tea kettle whistled, and he turned off the burner. As he fixed the cup of tea, a pair of grimy rubber boots lying by a door caught his eye. Odd, he thought. Had Catherine been wading in milk? The whitish stains looked fresh. He realized the door must lead to her garage, and he wondered why she'd left the dirty things on this side of the door, rather than in the garage.

Shrugging, he made a mental note to ask her if she wanted them in the garage. He also made a mental note to tell her that he would help her look for the codicil. That ought to cheer her up.

He wished he had stayed with her last night, though. She must have been sick all night. He'd panicked when he'd only been able to reach her answering machine earlier that morning. Then when he'd seen her pale face, guilt had hit him with a bang. Next time he'd let instinct rule, rather than Catherine. But in the meantime, he'd look after her. Besides, it felt kind of good.

He rummaged through her cabinets and refrigerator, looking for something suitable for her to eat, in case she was hungry. Not sure what a sick person should have, he got out an orange, some cold chicken, and a container of raspberry yogurt, then fixed a plate of Mallowmar cookies. He wondered if it was enough, and added two more cookies and a banana just to be sure.

"That ought to do it," he muttered, setting it all on a tray he'd found.

When he reentered her bedroom, every thought went clean out of his head.

Catherine was sitting up in the bed, the covers pulled to her waist. The heavy robe was gone and in its place was a lavender nightgown. The bodice was all lace, seductively hinting rather than blatantly displaying. A man could run his fingers down the spaghetti straps of the gown, then disperse with them in one quick flick. Her thick hair shone with reddish lights as it curved around her face and shoulders. Her skin was translucent, like fine porcelain. The last thing she looked was sick.

She stared back at him for a long moment, her eyes dark and unfathomable, then lifted the covers up to her chest in a casual manner. The spell over him deflated like a sagging balloon. He continued into her room and set the tray down on her lap.

Her eyebrows rose. "I thought I was getting a cup of tea."

"It's there." He pointed to the cup, then gingerly sat on the edge of the bed. Her legs were against his hip for one delicious second before she shifted them away. "I called my grandmother," he said. "She's coming over to take care of you."

Catherine's eyes widened, and she made a choking noise in the back on her throat. "Dammit, Miles, nobody gave you the right to do that!"

He raised his eyebrows. "What else was I supposed to do? You can't be alone when you're sick. Do you think you ought to have some medicine for that cough?"

"I am not coughing!"

Clearly, she was a crabby patient, he thought. He'd heard of this. She *had* coughed, though. "I think I'd better call a doctor—"

"No!" She shouted the word at him, the tray nearly tipping off her lap.

He rubbed his ear. "I'm not deaf. I was only making a suggestion, Catherine."

She lay back wearily on the propped up pillows. "Go run your bank, Miles. *Please*."

He frowned. "Aren't you going to eat anything?"

She scowled at him, her eyes blazing.

"I guess not," he muttered, getting up off the bed. He lifted the tray off her lap and set it on the nightstand for later. As he walked to the door, she called out to him.

"Miles."

He turned around. She smiled faintly, looking pale and lovely and vulnerable.

"Thank you."

He smiled. "You're welcome. Oh! I almost forgot. I've decided to help you find Allan's codicil."

She gasped. "You . . ."

He nodded, pleased to have surprised her. "Yes. I know some people I can call to track down that lawyer. Don't you worry, Catherine. I'll be in to see you tonight."

He left her still gaping in astonishment. At least her mind was off the flu.

"More goodies from Dr. Kitteridge."

Lettice waved a large white bag in the air as she swept into the bedroom. The name of the local pharmacy was emblazoned on the front. Catherine sighed and sank back on the bed. She hated playing invalid, but what else could she do?

Lettice opened the bag and spilled out ten different over-the-counter remedies. She glanced at Catherine. "I think he's trying to kill you."

"No kidding," Catherine muttered. He'd nearly given her heart attacks twice already that morning. The first time was when he'd showed up unexpectedly, and the second was over the codicil. What the hell did he mean, he would help her find it? Next to her uncle, he was the last person she thought would volunteer for such a thing.

He completely confused her. First, her disaster of an engagement didn't receive a single ounce of sympathy, then the very next morning he practically broke down her door because he thought she was sick. She wondered if he was up to something with the codicil. If he was, it wasn't to the good.

"Well, which poison do you want to take first?" Lettice asked.

Catherine didn't even glance at them. "None. I'm not that sick, Lettice. It was only a reaction to an old allergy of mine last night, and this morning I have a touch of the flu. Miles just went . . . nuts."

"Yes, I know, dear," Lettice said, smiling in pleasure. "It's very sweet of him."

Catherine conceded that the woman was right. She never would have expected Miles to fuss the way he had. And that tray of food . . . Nearly everything on it was exactly the wrong thing to give someone with a stomach illness. One glance and it would have sent the poor soul reeling to the bathroom. She grinned.

"You look pleased."

She sobered. "Just thinking. You don't have to stay, Lettice. I'm perfectly fine by myself."

"And have my grandson come down on me for going AWOL? In a pig's eye!"

Well, Catherine thought, it had been worth a try. She wondered how her dam was doing. When Miles had been waiting downstairs for his grandmother to arrive, she had made her phone calls. Anonymously, of course. Mariana Tolliver of Channel Five news had jumped on the call from "Earth Angel." What was happening there? Had everyone found the dam site? Were there enough pollutants already gathered? She desperately wanted to know. Her body was exhausted, but between the dam and Miles she was too keyed up to sleep. Besides, she had company that wasn't going anywhere fast.

"How about a game of canasta?" Lettice asked, as if having read her mind. "A dollar a point."

Catherine smiled. "You're on."

Miles saw Catherine much sooner than he'd expected.

He gaped at her as she strolled into the Wagner conference room for the second emergency meeting in two days. His grandmother was right behind her.

Catherine was dressed immaculately in a pale yellow suit. Her skin was healthy looking, not wan anymore, but the makeup didn't quite cover the drawn look she had. Although it was now late afternoon and she must have rested during the day, she still shouldn't be there.

He walked over to the women. "Catherine, go home. You're sick."

She merely raised her eyebrows. "I'm much better. How could I not be with all the food and medicine you gave me? Too bad you weren't around in the Middle Ages, Miles. You would have cured the plague single-handedly."

"Or killed its victims outright," Lettice added.

Catherine giggled and walked past him to speak to her relatives. Miles glared at his. "You are supposed to be taking care of her—"

"Why do you think I came with her?" his grandmother interrupted. "And if she's sick, then I'm Pee-Wee Herman. I lost four hundred dollars to her in canasta."

His jaw dropped. "Four hundred!"

"Don't look so shocked. Anyway, I'm donating it to the Green Earth Society. That was our agreement."

"Since we're all here," Byrne said loudly from the other end of the room, "we might as well get started. Lettice, you'll have to leave."

"In a pig's eye!" she declared, and defiantly took a seat opposite him. "Catherine isn't well, and I'm here to look after her."

Miles knew better. His grandmother simply hated to miss out on anything.

Byrne bristled. "I'll have security remove you if you won't go on your own—"

"And you are a pompous, overbearing nitwit," Lettice proclaimed. "Someone should have smacked a little common sense into you years ago."

Byrne gasped. "Why you—"

"Uncle Byrne," Catherine said calmly, "Lettice is hardly going to announce the proceedings to the world. I'd like her to stay, please."

"She stays," Miles announced, taking a seat next to Catherine. Her feminine perfume swirled around him, momentarily distracting him. These emergency meetings were becoming a nuisance, but her presence did make them bearable. More than bearable.

"Lettice knows everything anyway," Catherine added. "She was with me when Aunt Sylvia called about the meeting." She smiled innocently. "I might have missed it if Sylvia hadn't called. I take it the Earth Angel has struck again?"

Miles hid a smile at her subtle jab that she'd been left off the list of people to be called. His grandmother was right. With the way she was sitting forward in excitement, her slim body tensed with anticipation, she looked fully recovered. The angle at which she was leaning had her breasts just brushing the table top. Lucky table, he thought. He also had a feeling that she'd graduated from Corporate Strategy 101 a long time ago. She was working her uncle like a seasoned pro. He settled back to indulge his new favorite pastime, watching Catherine.

Byrne thrust out his jaw like a bulldog trying to exert its authority. It didn't work. "The nut blocked up the creek near our paint factory, then called the world."

"The EPA has found pollutants," Sylvia added. "It seems we had an old drainpipe that was broken and leaking waste by-products."

"It was an oversight," Byrne exclaimed. "Hadn't been inspected for years."

"What's the fine?" Miles asked, knowing the violation would be costly.

"They haven't said yet." He immediately changed the subject. "Now the media is really breathing down our necks."

"Then it's time to give a statement," Catherine said.

"We should have done it the last time," Miles added. She turned to look at him, and he grinned at her, feeling like they were a team. She was so close, all he had to do was reach out his hand and . . . He resisted the urge and went on, "Allan would have responded quickly. It's what we needed to do yesterday. It's what we need to do now."

"But what do we say?" Byrne wailed.

"That we are responsible," Catherine said, "and we will fix the 'leak' and ensure it never happens again." She looked around the table at the others. There was a slight knowing smile on her face as she added, "I think we'd be even better off if we announce several specific measures for improving the environment—"

"No!" Byrne shouted.

"Then Earth Angel will strike again."

Miles frowned. Something in Catherine's quiet declaration roused his suspicions. It wasn't a prediction, but rather more like . . . knowledge. A collage of images rose in his mind: Catherine wanting to find a codicil that would save land from becoming a strip mine, her push for environmental protection measures, her lack of surprise at the first meeting when everyone else was in a panic over Earth Angel. Accompanying the collage was the memory of boots with white stains and four hundred dollars to the Green Earth Society.

No, he thought, shaking the ridiculous notion out of his head. He believed the Earth Angel was someone at Wagner, but to even consider Catherine was ludicrous. She might be headstrong, but she wasn't foolish.

She rose from her chair. Miles knew she was about to make a grand exit. He liked this part best.

She again looked around at all of them. "This company must respond and must show good faith to the public concerning this latest incident. Otherwise we'll see Wagner Oil bankrupt. If that's what you want, then be stubborn. But I guarantee you won't stop the Earth Angel that way."

She shoved back her chair and walked out of the room. Lettice slowly rose from her own chair, smoothed out her skirt, then strolled out behind her patient. The Queen of England and Princess Diana couldn't have made a better exit, Miles thought.

If only his suspicions hadn't come back with a vengeance.

The iron had never been so hot, Catherine thought as she crawled under the fence. Her arms were trembling from the effort of pulling her body forward. This night promised as little sleep as the previous two. But she had to keep up the pressure.

Uncle Byrne was about to get a demonstration of the Earth Angel's power. The result should be heavenly.

Inexplicably, the idea of heaven instantly brought Miles to mind. She tried to shake off his image, but her brain refused to turn him loose. The way he had taken care of her when he'd thought she was sick had touched her more than she cared to admit. He had supported her at that meeting too. Both meetings. All of it was so unexpected . . . and she was so confused about him.

One thing she wasn't confused about was the way her body reacted to him. Having him next to her at the conference table had been almost too distracting. She had barely kept her concentration. Worse, she had found herself looking at his hands at every opportunity and remembering them on her body. Her breasts ached even now . . .

"Dammit!" she muttered, sitting up. She refused to think of him again, then she wondered why he hadn't come by that evening. He'd said he would.

She swore again, realizing how quickly she had broken her vow. She had better start concentrating on her objective for the night. She raced for it, a small blockhouse on the edge of the refinery. The night shift didn't work out this far, and the guards wouldn't be around for another thirty minutes. She wondered if they even knew what the blockhouse contained. She doubted her uncle remembered the emergency plant-closedown systems, established in case of a fire. But her uncle had reduced safety checks and crew to a bare minimum, and this little place was now overlooked.

"Ah, well," she murmured as she reached the little brick building. She used a key on the rusty lock and slipped inside. The door clanged shut behind her, and she whirled around. Fear shot through her at the thought that she was locked in. The key only worked from one side. She tested the knob and sighed when it turned.

Fixing her attention on the series of pipe valve shutoffs, she began the task of spinning them closed. She almost didn't have the strength to turn the big cast-iron wheels and struggled with the screeching metal. By the time she was done, she was shaking from head to toe. At least the second part was easy. She turned the smaller knobs on the system with a quick twist of the wrist, knowing they would trigger the shutoffs for this whole side of the plant. Instead of traveling through the piping system to the tankers on the river, the oil would stay safely in the tanks. They'd look everywhere for breakdowns before somebody remembered this.

"Ah, well," she murmured again, and walked to the door.

She opened it . . . and was face to face with Miles.

Five

"You—!"

Miles got as far as the first word in his furious tirade before Catherine burst out of the building.

"Not now, you idiot!" she whispered fiercely, shoving him out of the way as she ran past him. "The guards are coming!"

He stumbled backward, astonishment and outrage racing through him as fast as she was racing away. Somehow, he hadn't expected her to make a break for it.

To his further shock, she suddenly whipped around, dashed back, grabbed him by the arm, and yanked him forward. "Do you want to get caught as the Earth Angel? Come on!"

Miles ran automatically, her urgency overriding everything for a few vital seconds. Then he stiffened to a halt.

"Wait a damn minute!" he exclaimed.

Still holding his arm, Catherine was spun around automatically.

"Are you crazy?" he demanded. "How the hell can

you do this to your own company? And just what
the hell did you do? I want answers, and I want
them—"

"Miles, not now!" She was gasping for breath. In
the glare from the floodlights, her eyes were wide
and filled with genuine fear. She spun back toward
the fence fifty feet away and ran, calling over her
shoulder, "The guards will be here any second!
After we get out, I promise to explain. Now, *will
you come on!*"

He took off after her, determined to get her back
to undo whatever damage she had done. He could
not believe she was the Earth Angel. He had sat in
his car and watched her house all evening, still not
believing his suspicions. He had seen her car back
out of her garage at midnight, still not believing.
And he had followed her to the refinery, under the
fence, and to that little building, still not believing
what his eyes were seeing.

She reached the fence, lay on her stomach, and
scooted under the bent links in the blink of an eye.
Leaping to her feet, she lifted the jagged ends even
higher. "Come on!"

He set his jaw, then squirmed under the fence,
feeling the galvanized steel scrape his back and
legs. If his Saville Row suit survived all this, it
would be a tribute to his tailor. The moment he
stood up, Catherine grabbed his arm and pulled
him toward the darkness beyond the refinery's
perimeter lights.

As soon as they were swallowed by the night, she
let go of him and ran even faster. He instantly
realized that now she was trying to escape from
him. He leaped toward her, taking her down to the
uneven ground.

They hit it with a thud. As she yelped and struggled against him, he scrambled up until he was literally lying on top of her back, stretching her arms up above her head and effectively pinning her underneath him. She bucked and jerked futilely, and he rode her out. He couldn't quite ignore the primitive surge of conquest at her writhings, and struggled to remember this was about Earth Angel and Wagner Oil, and not about him and Catherine. Finally, she was still, her chest heaving with her exertions.

"Get off!" she gasped. "You weigh . . . a ton."

He lifted his body slightly to ease his weight . . . She instantly slid sideways, nearly getting out from under him. Cursing, he flattened himself on her again, his hips pressed tight against her derriere. His thigh was high between hers. He could feel the most intimate part of her . . .

"You're breaking your promise to explain," he said, desperate to shatter the sensual spell.

"So what?"

"Catherine, don't play games with me," he said wearily. "Clearly, you're the Earth Angel doing her little bit to save the world and thumb your nose at your family, all at the same time. Now what little bit did you do tonight in that building?"

"Nothing."

"Catherine."

"I never got a chance to do anything! You came along too fast. Okay?"

He wasn't that stupid, and it annoyed him that *she* thought he'd buy her story. At least she hadn't denied she was the Earth Angel. He would have felt even more insulted if she had.

"If you don't tell me," he said, "I swear I'll drag

you back into the refinery and stand over you until you fix whatever you've done."

She twisted her head to look at him. "Are you nuts? There are guards all over the place! I was lucky to get in and out of there once. And Miles, I don't think you want to be caught with the Earth Angel. Or haven't you thought about that yet?"

He admitted to himself that he hadn't. He also admitted he wouldn't even want to begin to explain his presence, or hers, to brawny security guards. "All right. We won't go back in. Just tell me what you've done, and I'll see it's corrected, somehow."

She snorted. "I told you I didn't do anything!"

He sensed he wouldn't get any information from her. She was too ready to be a martyr for the cause. Her first two escapades had been embarrassing but harmless. It looked like he would have to trust that this one was the same.

He remembered his overwhelming concern that morning when he'd thought she was alone and ill. Fury shot through him as he realized she must have been damming up that creek, not lying feverish in her bed. There he'd been feeling all . . . She had played him for a fool. Unfortunately, a deserted field in the dark was no place to force a confession. He had to have one answer, though.

"Just tell me why, Catherine."

"Why what?"

"Why you are doing this?"

"Why am I doing what?"

Something snapped inside him at her evasion. He was all too aware of the softness of her body and his need to have the upper hand with her, at least once. Muttering a curse under his breath, he pulled her to her feet and strode toward his car, keeping his arms wrapped tightly around her. Her feet dragged and stumbled, but he didn't stop.

"Miles, what are you doing?" she snapped, struggling against him.

"Taking you home."

They reached the two cars parked off the road by a pillar of the freeway overpass. He frowned at both of them, then made a decision. With one hand, he loosened his tie and whipped it off, somehow managing to keep Catherine pinned to his side. He used the strip of silk to tie her wrists together, both of them fighting all the way. Roping a two-ton Brahma bull had to be easier, he thought.

"I promise I won't run away again," she said when he was finally done.

"I suspect that promise is as good as the one about explaining everything once we got away from the plant." A devil rose up in him, and he pulled her closer. Raising her bound arms, he looped them around his neck. Her body pressed intimately against the length of his. He grinned. "This has great possibilities."

"Do you feel all nice and macho now?" she asked, glaring at him.

He backed her against his car. "Don't tempt me, Catherine."

Her gaze never wavered. Even in the darkness he could sense the challenge radiating out of her. That coupled with the feel of her body against his was almost too much for his willpower. She would kill a weak man, and she damn near broke him. He sensed their anger would quickly turn to passion for both of them if he so much as kissed her now. But afterward, she would absolve herself with the excuse that he'd overwhelmed her by being "macho." He wanted Catherine, but not now, not like this.

He ducked his head out from under her hands, his chin brushing along her breasts. Her nipples were diamond hard even through the sweater she was wearing. He wondered how stupid he could be, then opened the passenger door.

"Get in the car," he said between clenched teeth.

"But what about mine?"

"I'll have someone pick it up."

"But—"

He pushed her inside, then locked and shut the door. Once in the driver's seat, he started the car and backed it out onto the dirt road.

"All right," Catherine said. "I'll play prisoner until we get to my house—"

"My house."

He liked the way she gasped.

"I am not going to your house," she announced.

He grinned. "Who's driving?"

"Miles, this is ludicrous!"

"No more ludicrous than your being the Earth Angel. You have been playing a dangerous game, and it's going to stop before you get hurt. I've decided that tonight was Earth Angel's swan song. And you'll be staying with me so I can ensure it."

She gasped again, this time in pure outrage.

He smiled to himself.

Life definitely had its moments.

Catherine watched Miles as he pulled the curtains shut in his study, then checked the messages on his answering machine. His dark hair, usually so stiffly brushed back, was tousled by their fighting, and the front locks fell across his forehead. She realized she was getting a glimpse of what he'd looked like as a young boy. She turned away quickly, refusing to admit how endearing he looked. Considering how he'd treated her, the last thing she should be feeling was attracted to him. She yanked on her hands once more, but he'd firmly tied them to a drawer of his filing cabinet, forcing her to sit on the floor with her back to the cabinet.

"You have no right to do this!" she told him for what seemed like the hundredth time.

"I suppose not," he agreed. "But you had no right to do whatever you did at the refinery."

"Come on, Miles," she said, trying a wheedling tone. "You don't really mean this. Think of what the neighbors would say if they saw this."

He smiled grimly. "They'd say hurrah for taking care of public enemy number one."

She scrunched her backside around on the Persian carpet and licked her lips. Her body was sweaty, her clothes were filthy, and her hair was hanging in stringy hanks around her face. If she was going to be stuck sitting on the floor tied to a filing cabinet, she ought to be comfortable. And clean.

"Can I take a shower?" she asked.

"Anytime you want," he said. "Of course, I'll have to wash you. You won't be able to do it properly with your hands tied. I'm ready, willing, and very able to help you."

"Thank you, but no," she said curtly. "Miles, this is absolutely ridiculous."

"Probably. But I can't let you loose to play Earth

Angel anytime you please. And you've already proven I can't trust a promise from you."

She made a face. "You can't keep me here forever."

"The thought is appealing." He sat down on the floor next to her, and every muscle in her body tensed at his closeness. "You've been having fun poking at the family because they won't listen to you. But sooner or later, you'll go too far and somebody will get hurt. And that someone will be you."

She stared at him. He sounded so sincere, as if he really cared about what happened to her. She shook her head sharply, tossing away the silly thought. His "concern" was no doubt motivated by fear of the scandal that might erupt if the press found out she was Earth Angel. The headlines would be a corporate and personal embarrassment to him.

"Are you going to turn me in to Byrne?"

"Hardly." He chuckled dryly. "I think you wouldn't mind that at all right now. No, you'll be my guest for a while—at least until you confess what you've done tonight."

"I already told you—"

"And I don't believe you."

She set her lips together and just gazed at him, silent.

"How lovely to have you with me for an extended stay, Catherine. I'm hungry. Catching earth angels sure works up an appetite. Want something?"

She shook her head, privately deciding to go on a hunger strike until he let her go. A day of watching her starve ought to send him into a panic. He'd release her in no time.

"Okay," he said, and got up.

"I want my own room," she said.

He grinned wickedly. "Only if it's mine."

"Miles!" she screeched at him, but he calmly walked out of the room.

This was only supposed to happen in pirate stories, she thought, frustration and panic running through her. She felt too much like a heroine helplessly trussed to a pirate king's bed. So when did Errol Flynn come crashing through the window to rescue her? No time soon, she bet. Instead, she was at the mercy of Miles Kitteridge.

She closed her eyes and shuddered. He was just trying to scare her with this prisoner business, she told herself. He really didn't mean to keep her until she confessed. He couldn't. He would probably only keep her until the morning to put the fear of Miles into her.

She leaned her head back, weary from the lack of sleep, weary from wrestling in the dirt with him, and weary from the aftermath of tension. She was worried about her car too. That wasn't the best place to abandon a vehicle for any length of time.

What frightened her the most was being alone with Miles. Turning her in to the family wasn't the worst thing he could do to her. Sitting close to her, touching her, that was the worst he could do. She knew all of her anger would melt away if he showed her the slightest tenderness, gave her the lightest kiss. She was simply much too vulnerable with him.

She would just have to stay awake, she vowed. Very awake.

•   •   •

Miles walked back into the study, carefully balancing a loaded tray.

"I brought you some cheese and crackers," he began, then looked up. Catherine was sound asleep, her head back between her arms. "But I guess you're not hungry."

He set the tray on a small table, then picked up a bottle of beer and an apple. Settling onto the sofa, he said, "You're missing one heck of a snack."

A very faint, very genuine snore answered him.

"Thank you for that editorial comment."

He took a sip of beer, then a bite of the apple, the bitter and the tastes clashing in his mouth.

Just like Catherine, he thought.

Catherine slowly surfaced from a black void.

Soft sweet kisses brushed along her cheek, her jaw. Enticing lips grazed hers, strayed away, then returned, teasing and tormenting. She sighed as the kiss deepened, those wonderful lips moving over hers in a rhythm that swirled through her senses. Tongues mated in a slow, sensual dance. Strong hands caressed her back, the curve of her hip. She tried to reach up and embrace her dream lover, but she couldn't move her hands . . .

The night came back with a vengeance.

Her eyes snapped open to meet Miles's amused gaze. She scooted away from the warm hard body next to hers, but she didn't scoot far.

Her tied wrists jerked her back. She was no longer tied to the file cabinet. Instead, she was tied to Miles, her two wrists to one of his. They were lying together, pressed disconcertingly close, on his couch.

"Good morning," he said cheerfully.

"Miles, you son of a—"

"Tsk, Catherine. Such language."

She glared at him. "I didn't get to say it yet."

"But you will."

"You bet." Her head was full and pounding as if she had a bad hangover. She desperately wanted to yell and scream her frustrations at him, but she refused to appear anything but calm and cool in front of him. "Miles, I cannot believe you are doing this."

He ran his forefinger down her cheek. "I know. Brilliance comes along only once in a lifetime. Maybe twice. Do you remember when I asked you into my bed?"

She wasn't likely to forget, not now. The scent of him, musky and unique, surrounded her. The warmth and strength of his body was a magnet pulling her closer. Holding herself still against the sensual shiver that threatened to run through her, she said, "Yes."

"And here you are tied to me." He smiled. "Not exactly how I expected things to work, but we did spend the night together."

"I'm thrilled to my toes. By the way, are you planning to leave me tied up and alone for the rest of the day while you're at the bank?"

"If I have to, I will. Or maybe I'll ask Grandmother to come over and watch you again."

"Lettice would let me go," she said triumphantly.

He chuckled. "You don't know my grandmother very well. This is the kind of thing that would tickle her."

He sounded so sure, she wondered if he was right. As she gazed at him, she knew he was prepared to go on with this absurd charade for days. And she wouldn't be able to take even another morning of this. Feeling defeated, she asked, "What will it take, Miles?"

His humor vanished, and his gaze searched hers. "What did you do last night?"

She hesitated, then finally answered, "All I will say is that it will be annoying but it won't hurt anybody."

"Not good enough."

"Then we're at an impasse."

"I can take it." He ran his hand up and down her arm, sending signals of delight throughout her body.

"You can't leave me alone in the house," she said desperately, all too aware of their cramped space. "What if there's a fire?"

"I told you, I'll get my grandmother to watch you."

"Isn't there another way?"

He thought for a moment, his hand blessedly stilling.

"I don't know," he said slowly. "If I could trust your word—"

"I do have some integrity, you know," she snapped. "I will honor any agreement you and I make."

"I almost believe you."

"Miles."

He sighed. "I don't suppose Grandmother would babysit forever. Will you confess?"

"No. It wouldn't do you any good anyway. You could never explain how you knew without everyone thinking you're in cahoots with Earth Angel."

"I'm lying on a couch with her, actually." He smiled thoughtfully. "You have a point, though."

"Well, since you're willing to compromise, I suppose I should too."

He nodded. "So you'll agree to stay with me and not run away?"

"Live here?" Her voice was a squeak of alarm. She cleared her throat.

"Someone has to watch over you."

"I'm not a child."

His hand slid up her arm and around her shoulder. He pulled her closer. "No," he murmured, "you're not a child."

She craned her head back as his lips grazed her neck. "Not like this, Miles. How good is your word?"

"My word is perfect," he said, backing off slightly in effront.

She hid her sigh of relief, thinking madly. The shut valves would be discovered in a day or two at the most, and she wouldn't have to confess anything. Still, she preferred not to spend that time trussed up in Miles's house. "Then let's see how perfect it is. I'll agree not to escape if you agree to be a perfect gentleman."

He frowned at her. "I'm not sure I like your terms."

"And I don't like yours, so we're even."

"How long?"

"I'll stay until they discover Earth Angel's latest exploit."

"Done."

He had taken the bargain so fast, she wondered

if he saw a loophole she didn't. The thought was frightening.

"I'll untie you and you'll come to the office with me," he said. "In fact, everywhere I go, you will go." He grinned. "You'll make a big splash in the executive washroom."

"I just promised I wouldn't escape!" she exclaimed.

He pulled her to him, crushing her breasts against his chest. "I simply want a little reassurance over the next few days, okay? After your performance last night—"

"All right!" Anything to get untied and away from his body, she thought. She didn't trust herself with him.

He released her. "Spoilsport."

"Could I be untied now?" she asked. "I haven't wet my pants since I was five, and I'd like to keep that record."

He scowled. "You know how to kill a mood too."

She smiled happily. "Thank you."

Miles signed the stack of letters his secretary had left on his desk, all the time acutely conscious of Catherine sitting on his office sofa. She was curled up with a book, the picture of complete innocence. He knew better.

He could just imagine the rumors spreading throughout the bank about her being in his office. His secretary had been in and out four times so far that morning on minor stuff, wanting to peek at his visitor. Personally, he didn't care what anyone's speculations were, and Catherine seemed oblivious to it.

So far she had kept her word. She had preferred to shower and change clothes in her town house, and he had waited patiently through the process, half braced for her to attempt to escape. She hadn't. In fact, she had come down with a bag packed, clearly ready to fulfill their bargain.

The thought of her attached to his hip twenty-four hours a day started his blood pounding. He doubted if he would tire of her for a single minute. Even now, just knowing she was there did things to his system that excited and soothed him at the same time. Viking princes must have felt the same when they took a prized captive back home.

He must be going nuts, he thought. For all the trouble Catherine caused, he couldn't understand why he felt so damned good at the moment. Maybe he didn't want to know.

"By the way," he said. She looked up from her book, and he went on, "I haven't gotten an answer yet from my friend on who your grandfather made his will with. But it will turn up."

She smiled obliquely. "And when it does, will I actually get to see it? Or will it disappear into the mists?"

"Don't be prickly, Catherine," he warned, suppressing his irritation at her questions. "I have yet to break my word, unlike you."

She had the grace to flush before she turned back to her book.

He resisted the urge to apologize. There was nothing he needed to apologize for, dammit. Anyway, he didn't want to fight with her. He only wanted her.

He had promised to be a gentleman, but he

hadn't promised to resist her if she tried to seduce him. He smiled. Confessions and codicils be damned. He knew what he wanted, and a little wooing just might get it for him. A perfectly legitimate loophole in their agreement. He was batting three for three in brilliant ideas.

And once Catherine was in his bed, he doubted he'd ever let her out of it again.

The words on the page blurred together as Catherine got a wonderfully wicked idea.

She couldn't, she thought.

Yes, she could, a little voice told her. She had only agreed not to run away. *But* she hadn't agreed not to do any more Earth Angel missions. She could go out, do one, and come back, and not break the agreement they had. It was a legitimate loophole, so what could Miles do?

Probably kill her anyway.

She glanced at him out of the corner of her eye. His head was bent over his work, the thick dark hair perfectly groomed as always. Under that urbane appearance, though, was a rock hard man who twisted her in knots.

"Miles, my car," she said, suddenly remembering he had taken her keys the night before to have it moved. "Where's my car?"

"At my housekeeper's house. Her husband went and got it for me. They'll bring it around to the house today. Why?"

"I wondered if you remembered it."

He grinned smugly. "Yes, I managed, despite all the excitement you provide."

It would be lovely to outwit him, she thought. "Please thank them for me."

"Of course."

He went back to his work, and she made a decision.

Earth Angel would strike again.

Six

"I want my own bedroom."

Miles had been expecting this request all evening. In fact, he was very surprised Catherine hadn't made it before the eleven o'clock news.

She turned in her chair and looked at him. Her expression was carefully polite and completely stubborn. "I want my own bedroom, Miles, or all bargains are off."

"I never said I wouldn't give one to you," he said in a mild tone. What was going on inside him was hardly mild, though. Having her in any bedroom but his own was the last thing he wanted. Unfortunately, about halfway through the day he'd realized that there was a major flaw in their bargain. Still, if he didn't give in on this point, she would be gone in an instant. "Go pick your room."

"Thank you." She stood up and stretched.

Miles choked back a groan as she arched her back, thrusting her breasts forward. His hands ached to flow over her curves, to entice her soft nipples into seductive points, to discover the tautness of her waist, the cradle of her hips . . .

"I'll come with you," he said, standing up.

She turned around. "I can be trusted to find myself a bedroom."

He grinned. "I was lonely without you."

"I hadn't gone yet."

"It was the thought, Catherine. Besides, a good host should show a guest around."

"I'm not your guest. I'm your prisoner."

"A good warden should ensure that no Geneva Convention agreements on prison conditions are being broken."

"You're a paladin of comedians, Miles," she said dampeningly, and strode out of the room.

Miles followed happily. Macho men had no idea what they were missing by having women walk behind them, he mused. Men belonged behind women, drooling in pleasure. He also understood Petruchio's need to see a moment of softness in Shakespeare's Katherine. He'd love to see one in his own. Just one minute shift in her attitude toward him and he would find himself . . .

He instantly turned his mind away from the disturbing thought of how his own feelings toward her would change. He wasn't sure he was ready to face that.

Upstairs, he finally stepped ahead of her to show her the bedrooms. He opened the first door on a front bedroom. "It's a nice little room, but it faces the street."

"The street has to be a hundred yards away," Catherine said. "I doubt three cars go down it at night, way out here in the country." She walked inside to check the neutral decor, then turned back. "This is fine."

No, it wasn't, he thought. It was too far from his bedroom. "See the rest before you decide."

He took her arm and pulled her out into the hallway, leading her to the next room. He pronounced it unfit. She inspected it anyway. Two more bedrooms brought the same result, but an unexpected question.

"Miles, why do you have such a big house?" she asked, looking puzzled.

He shrugged. "It seemed the thing to do when I got married."

"You kept it? Not your wife?"

"She preferred the wilds of Palm Beach. It's a good investment."

She shook her head. "Don't you have something just because you like it and damn the money?"

He thought about it for a moment. "I doubt it."

Snorting, she moved to the next door. It was open. "That one's already occupied," Miles said. "Sorry."

He began to escort her past the door, eager to get to the bedroom beyond. It was next to his own, and the only acceptable one.

Catherine halted and went back to the open door, saying, "What do you mean 'it's occupied'?"

Without waiting for an answer, she walked inside. He reached the door just as she flipped on the light switch. Sprawled on the bed was a white Persian cat. The animal raised its head, watching them.

"I didn't know you had a cat," Catherine said, looking at him speculatively.

"That's Sheba," he said. "As in Queen of, because she thinks she is one. You haven't had the opportunity to meet her yet. She sleeps in here sometimes."

"You give a cat her own bedroom?"

"No one else is using it." He shrugged, feeling oddly sheepish. Sheba did what she pleased most of the time, and he'd learned not to waste his breath with her years ago.

"Is she friendly?"

"Not very."

The cat had been licking her paws during the conversation, but paused as Catherine walked over to the bed. Sheba looked at her, blinked in unconcern, then went back to her washing. She didn't move when Catherine reached out and stroked her head. She didn't purr, either.

Catherine straightened. "I'll stay in this room."

"But this is Sheba's room!" Miles said, gaping at her.

"We'll share."

He shook his head. "Sheba won't tolerate it."

"She'll just have to." Catherine smiled and took his arm, escorting him to the door.

The feel of her fingers on his arm, the scent of her perfume, and the closeness of her body was all too much for him. He stopped and turned to her, bringing her against him. Her lips parted in surprise. He leaned forward and kissed them, tasting the sweetness she always hid and the sensuality she couldn't hide.

Her mouth softened, then kissed him with a hunger that sent his senses spinning. He was ready to forget all bargains.

"This isn't a good room for you," he murmured against her lips. "There's another room, just down the hall—"

She pulled her head back, her eyes wary even as her breasts heaved against his chest. "Your room."

"Yes." He tugged her toward him, wanting the softness back. "Catherine . . ."

She pushed him out the door, then shut it. "Good night, Miles."

He stared at the stained and varnished wood that barred him from the two females in his life. "Catherine, Sheba isn't a nice cat."

No answer.

"Catherine, there are five other bedrooms to choose from. You don't have to take Sheba's room or the one I suggested before." It killed him to say it, but he did. "Or mine . . ."

No answer.

"Catherine, this is silly."

He realized he was wasting his breath. She was going to do what she pleased.

Just like the cat.

Stripped down to her undergarments, Catherine lay in the bed and stared across the darkness to the white lump perched on the bedroom chair. She had no doubt Sheba was staring back in fury.

The cat's initial tolerance of her had vanished the moment she'd sat on the bed. Sheba had hopped off instantly with a snarl of anger. The cat had paced in front of the door, then at last had taken up her baleful watch on the small upholstered chair. So much for a friendly face, Catherine thought. Still, she wasn't about to let the cat out for Miles to discover. She wondered if the creature was yet another investment. Sheba was clearly a champion-bred feline. Did he show her?

Probably. He probably overbred her, too, to get every bit of profit he could from her. So why was she so attracted to him? And how had she managed to shut the door in his face?

Catherine stifled a moan at the thought of being alone with him in the house. She had recognized that he was leading her closer and closer to his bedroom. What would he have done? Offered her his room, then wandered in all night long "for a few things I forgot"? She could imagine what would have happened, because she did not for one minute trust her control. She knew Miles would never break his word, but he certainly wouldn't stop *her* if things got out of hand. She had been too close to him all day. She had watched the way he smoothed down his tie and remembered his hands smoothing their way down her body. She had gazed at his mouth and wished he were spreading kisses on every inch of her skin. The scent of him had drifted to her often, constantly triggering a reaction deep inside her.

He had been charming and solicitous all evening. David Niven would have been envious of his perfect-gentleman performance—even down to the flowers at her place at dinner. Violets. How had he known she liked violets? It had been all she could do to sit in the same room with him after that. She had tried to remind herself that he had caused her great embarrassment over her wedding, but somehow all she could think of was that he'd done her a favor. She had known then that she needed some peace that night, or she would explode.

Even now her muscles ached with the urge to get up and walk down that hall to him. Her heart sang

with the thought that she was where she belonged. Belonged . . .

What was wrong with her? Why was she reacting
this way to him? And why had she agreed to this
ridiculous captor/captive scenario? She avoided
that question all day, but now, lying alone in the
dark, she forced herself to face it.

She had too much pride and, if she were honest,
too much fear of Miles's power over her to come to
him openly and reveal her deep attraction to him.
She could have walked out of his office any time
that day, and in front of all those people, he
couldn't have stopped her. More than her integrity
had kept her there, though. Pure and simple, she
hadn't wanted to leave him. She was playing with
fire, but deep inside she admitted that, while she
didn't want to get burned, she wouldn't mind
sharing his heat. That was why she'd agreed to the
bargain, that was why she was still there. As much
as she might deny it to anyone else, she could no
longer lie to herself. She was falling in love with
Miles Kitteridge.

From his corner of the breakfast nook, Miles
watched Catherine walk hesitantly into the
kitchen.

She looked oddly vulnerable in a denim skirt and
red-checked blouse, like the girl next door that a
boy never fooled around with—until he came back
from college and fell in love with her.

He should have come back from college and
fallen in love with Catherine.

The thought was disturbing. He pushed it aside,
and pushed aside as well the memory of the restless

night he'd spent listening for footsteps in the hall-way, marking an escape; and resisting the urge to go into Sheba's room, which would have marked him as a cad. About three in the morning, he had been willing to prove himself one. Very willing.

"Good morning," he said.

Catherine turned around at the sound of his voice, but didn't answer. Her expression pensive, even almost wary, she walked over to the table and sat down opposite him, at the place he'd set for her. She picked up the coffee pot and poured herself a cup, then took a sip. Finally she said, "Good morning."

"At last." He handed her a covered basket. "Muffin?"

"Thank you."

"There are eggs and bacon in the warmer." He tapped the large covered tray on the table between them. "I made them."

Her eyebrows rose. "Interesting. By the way, Sheba made you a present upstairs."

"She made me . . . ?" He scowled as realization dawned.

Catherine lifted the warmer lid and dug herself out a large helping. "I'm not cleaning it up. She's your cat."

"This wouldn't have happened if you'd taken another bedroom."

"Or if you let me go home."

"I'll clean it up," he muttered.

She chuckled.

"Well, well, well," a voice exclaimed with great satisfaction. "Does this signify a truce in the proceedings?"

Miles glanced up to see his grandmother walking into the kitchen. He set his jaw and looked over at Catherine, who was flushed the color of her blouse. There went the intimate breakfast with her, he thought, and vowed to take away his grandmother's house key.

He rose as she reached the table. "Don't get your gossip motor running, Grandmother. Catherine is just having a power breakfast with me about some things at Wagner Oil."

How he wished it was different.

"And did you have a power night?" Lettice asked.

"Hardly," he muttered, glancing over at Catherine.

"Oh, poop," Lettice said, accepting his kiss.

Catherine giggled, thinking of Sheba's little gift. "Actually," she said to Lettice, "Miles is keeping me a prisoner."

"That's my grandson." She patted him on the back, but it was obvious she didn't believe a word of it. Miles didn't know whether to laugh at his grandmother's innocence or at Catherine's look of disappointment, so he just smiled to himself. He doubted Catherine would say anything about Earth Angel, and he was right. She went back to her eggs.

"I stopped by on my way to a charity meeting to discuss some business with you," Lettice said. "So can a third party join the power breakfast? I won't be long. Mamie's waiting for me in the car."

Miles pulled out a chair. "Of course."

Catherine stood as Lettice sat. "I'll leave you two."

"Sit," Lettice ordered. "My business isn't secret, and I trust you, anyway. Sit, Miles."

He and Catherine sat at the same time.

"Very nice," his grandmother murmured, then launched into a discussion about whether or not she should invest in a small resort a friend of hers wanted to buy.

Miles was dubious. Catherine was adamantly against it. Evidently, she knew the friend better than he did.

"I'll tell Bunny no, then," Lettice said, finishing her shredding of a blueberry muffin. The fruit lay in a little pile on the side of the bread plate. "Now, what did I interrupt?"

"Just a bargain Miles and I have made over my grandfather's will," Catherine said before he could answer.

Lettice smiled. "What bargain?"

Miles was wondering the same thing.

"Miles has some people trying to trace the lawyer Grandfather used," Catherine said. "He's promised to turn it over to me to file, rather than my uncle."

"I wouldn't think you'd need a promise for that," Lettice said.

Neither did Miles.

Catherine shrugged, not looking at him. "I'm grateful for it, though. Now I *know* the codicil won't conveniently disappear."

Although his grandmother chuckled, Miles realized that Catherine still didn't trust him and had brought the bargain up in front of a witness to ensure he wouldn't renege. Anger instantly rose, and just as instantly it subsided. He supposed he would be suspicious if he were her.

Breakfast was quickly disposed of, and his grandmother left for her charity meeting. Miles was tempted to let his housekeeper take care of Sheba's mess, but it didn't seem fair. He took care of it himself, holding his breath the entire time. Catherine left him to it, not quite smothering a grin. He vowed the bedroom arrangements would be radically changed that night.

"All finished?" she asked him when he joined her in the garage.

He set his briefcase and jacket on the hood of the BMW, then rolled down his sleeves. "Thank you, yes."

"That cat really has a revenge streak, doesn't she?"

He set his jaw. "Probably she was shut up in the room, when she needed to get out."

"Nah." Catherine shook her head and folded her arms across her chest. "She had a look of satisfaction on her face this—"

Miles opened the car door. "Get in."

She giggled and began to slip past him into the seat. The sound of her carefree, mischievous laugh made his heart flip over. He reached out and stopped her. That touch, her closeness, her teasing, and the night with her under his roof nearly undid him.

He pulled her to him, his mouth brushing hers lightly. "Catherine . . ."

"You promised." Her voice was thin and reedy, as if she were miles away, instead of every inch of her pressed to him. Her flesh seemed to burn his fingers. His breathing was raspy. The unique perfume of her numbed his mind, wiping away everything but the desire to taste her sweetness, to feel her in his arms. It had come on him so fast. No other woman but Catherine could do this to him.

"Break my promise for me," he whispered, her lips a scant inch from his. He had only to press lightly, and he would possess her mouth again. "You want to. I want you to."

"No." The denial was as threadbare as a poor man's cloak.

"I want you with me the way you should be." His lips not touching hers was torture. "There's more than a bargain between us, Catherine. Just be with me."

A faint moan erupted from the back of her throat. "You promised. Miles . . ."

Was his name an enticement or a protest? Virtue finally penetrated his numb brain. He lifted his head and stared at her. She was breathing as heavily as he.

"You promised," she managed to repeat.

He cursed her iron will and let her go.

"Why, Catherine?" he asked. "You want this as much as I do."

"Because I don't go to bed with a man just because he's attractive," she answered.

"Progress," he said in a caustic tone. "I never thought I'd hear those words from you."

She stared at him for a long moment, then got into the car. He slammed the door shut behind her.

He was sick to death of the damn bargain.

Opportunity knocked that night for Catherine. Or rather, it rang the doorbell.

Miles glanced up from his papers when he heard it, then glanced at his watch. "I was afraid of that."

"Of what?" Catherine asked, wondering if another dinner party was about to descend. They'd already eaten.

His housekeeper, Mrs. Truman, came into the living room. "It's George Harmon."

Miles set the papers aside and stood up. "Take him into the study. I'm sorry, Catherine, but this will take awhile. A deal George and I are putting together has some bugs in it."

She hoped they were the size of swamp rats, as Earth Angel's timetable was now bumped up by several hours. It was a small mission, but an important one, and she had wondered how she'd get away to do it. Now she knew. She smiled consolingly at Miles.

"Don't worry about me. I'm sure you've provided plenty of prison entertainment. I'll watch a movie. Maybe *Wall Street* or *Pretty Woman*. Both have ruthless businessmen. It'll be like you're right here with me."

He didn't appreciate her humor. "Just behave yourself, and no escaping."

"I wouldn't dream of it," she vowed, wishing he'd unbend a little. He'd been stiff with her all day, ever since the incident by the car that morning. A small part of her was relieved, but most of her was disappointed. That worried her.

"Catherine," he said in warning.

"Miles," she said, imitating his tone. Then she sighed. "I will not break our bargain."

He nodded. "Good enough."

He left the room. She sat perfectly still and listened to the men's voices fading down the hallway.

Catherine waited impatiently for nearly twenty minutes. When she felt sure the men were deep in their deal, she was out of the room and up the stairs like a quiet bullet. Sheba didn't even have time to blink as she raced past the cat, grabbing her purse and jacket. Miles, bless his heart, had given her back her keys that evening in a show of trust. Guilt rose in her like a tidal wave. She forced it away. He could trust her not to break her promise. She was just going to bend it a little.

Her compact was parked outside the garage. She wondered briefly if it was there because there was no more room in the garage, or if it didn't rate with his high-class cars.

"Who cares," she muttered.

Once inside the car, she shoved the key in the ignition. At least now she didn't have to creep through the house in the wee hours and chance Miles discovering her. That would be dangerous.

Then again, so was this.

She shrugged and started the car.

Earth Angel was going for a little ride.

Miles heard the motor through the open study window. Something told him it wasn't Mrs. Truman leaving for the night.

He whipped his chair out from under the desk and leaped to the window, just in time to see the back lights of Catherine's car wind around the curve of the circular drive.

He blinked, positive he was not seeing what he was seeing.

The car lights winked at him as they disappeared into the night.

"Meeting's over. Have to go," he gasped, running for the door. He had a brief glimpse of George's O of astonishment as he shot past him.

Within seconds, he was in the 'Vette and turning

over the engine. Precious seconds were lost as the automatic garage door opener took its usual sweet time. He finally gave vent to a string of curses, which didn't even begin to take the edge off his towering fury.

Catherine had broken her promise.

All bargains were off.

Catherine pulled off to the side of the street and parked her car high on the shoulder under a tree to make it look like a breakdown. She shut off the engine and sat for a moment watching the cars go by. Not a single Samaritan among them, thank goodness.

Most people passing the wooded area probably thought the trees were a small overgrown copse just within the city limits. She knew the truth. Wagner Oil was dumping drums of illegal waste chemicals in the landfill just beyond the trees.

When she finally left her car, she took a flashlight and a large sign with her, one she had made several days ago. She slipped through the trees and undergrowth, careful of the broken concrete under her feet. This was a dump all right.

Flipping on the flashlight, she checked around the site. Mostly it was concrete rubble and broken glass in a makeshift landfill. But there were also tires, bikes, and even an abandoned car. And it was dark, and she was alone. Her nerves skittered, and her stomach jumped in anxiety. Just set up the sign and get out, she told herself.

She'd actually be glad to be back at Miles's house after this.

• • •

Miles sat in his car and stared ahead, unblinking. He was parked about two hundred yards back from Catherine. He had managed to catch up with her on the country roads by his home, and he'd kept her in sight ever since. She'd stopped at her town house, parking her car on the street instead of in her garage. He'd decided to sit tight and wait for her, and sure enough, she had come out again, carrying a sheet of wood almost as big as she was.

It wasn't hard to guess what she was up to, and his fury had returned tenfold. She did this after the way he had trusted her, after the way he was beginning to . . .

He'd nearly lost her in the city, and had been relieved when she finally stopped. He'd watched her get out of her car, then wrestle the sign from the back. A few cars went by, but not a soul stopped. The area around the refinery had been dangerous enough at night, but this place . . .

Miles pulled the 'Vette completely off the road, steering the vehicle behind some bushes for protection. Then he got out of the car and followed her.

Catherine heard someone scrambling over the broken glass and concrete behind her and immediately dropped the sign she'd been trying to shove into the packed earth. It fell with a bang as she whipped around. She screamed at the noise, and at the sight of someone running toward her. She turned and tried to scramble to safety.

"Catherine!"

She stumbled and turned, her flashlight's beam picking up a familiar person in its light.

"Miles!" she gasped, her heart racing half in relief and half in fear. "You're supposed to be in a meeting!"

His expression was thunderous, anger radiating out of him like an overheated car. "I canceled it. We had a bargain, Catherine."

"And I was keeping it," she said, her breath coming hard and fast.

"This is not keeping it!" he roared.

"Miles, relax. I was just putting up the sign and then I was coming back. And keep your voice down, will you?"

She walked back to the sign, which had survived the scare, then bent down and began scraping at the iron-hard dirt, using a stick for a shovel.

"I will not keep my voice down!" he shouted, striding over to her and yanking her to her feet.

A thread of fear whipped through her at his murderous expression. Maybe she had pushed things a little too far this time. In an effort to calm him, she said, "Miles, honest, I wasn't breaking the bargain to escape. I promised I wouldn't, and I meant it. But I didn't promise I wouldn't do any more Earth Angel missions. I would never promise that, and you know it."

"But you knew that's what I meant, dammit!"

"Then you should have said it."

He almost exploded. "Catherine!"

"Miles, look at these drums here."

She shone the flashlight on several drums half buried in the dirt. Rust was already eating at the metal. He glanced at them. "So? They're drums."

"Not just any drums, Miles. They're filled with

waste chemicals from Wagner Oil. The plant is right over there." She pointed toward faint lights far off across the empty field. "They've been secretly burying these here for the last four months."

He stared at her, then at the drums. "But they look years old."

She could feel the shock run through him. Complacent Miles was getting a rude awakening. "*Months* old. They're already leaching out the waste into the ground under the fill. A developer will no doubt buy this lot some day, if one hasn't already. And of course, the mess will be discovered then. But the culprit won't be. There's nothing to trace Wagner here . . . except Earth Angel. I *have* to do this. For my grandfather. I'll be back at your house when I'm done. Just as I promised."

She knelt down and began poking at the earth again.

Miles knelt next to her. "Catherine, these signs and pranks are not the way to stop this. It's dangerous to be out at night alone—especially in this place. Go to the . . . Here, give me that." He took the stick from her struggling hands. His scraping was much more effective than hers. "Go to the family—"

"I did. A month ago, I told my father what Byrne's been doing. He called me a liar."

"No comment about your father."

"I've already said it anyway." She watched him dig, trying not to smile. His mouth might be saying the wrong things, but his hands were doing the right ones. She would keep this picture of Miles in her heart always.

"Go straight to the EPA," he said, "and report—"

"I did that too. But they take forever to act,

Miles, even if they think the complaint is a legitimate one. I called them anonymously, which was my fatal mistake. Earth Angel is newsworthy, and once the media is in on it, then bureaucracy moves a whole lot faster to cover the embarrassment and look good to the public."

"You could have come to me—"

"No, I couldn't," she snapped, angry with his obtuse suggestion. "You wouldn't have believed me, either, and you know it. I'm Catherine the idealist, Catherine the alarmist, Catherine the hippie. Nobody believes me because they think I'm against anything that makes a profit. Well, I like the money fine, but let's do it right, even if it means a little less profit. And let's not break the law for a buck, okay?"

"Okay." He threw down the stick and sat back on his heels. "This dirt is too damn hard. Let's get some of the concrete to prop the sign up instead."

"Very bright, Miles."

She held the sign while he propped concrete blocks around it. She smiled in amusement the entire time. He was wonderful.

He glanced up. "What are you staring at?"

"You," she said. "Just you."

"Oh."

As she stood next to him, she was aware of everything about him. The strength in his hands, the way his hair fell over his forehead, the intense energy within him. Emotions that ran the gamut from excitement to tenderness washed through her heart.

As he set the last block in place, he said, "Never *ever* do this again, Catherine."

She smiled innocently. "I won't do a sign again."

"No. No more Earth Angel."

She just looked at him.

"We'll discuss this at home."

She just looked at him.

He sighed and started walking toward the road. "Come on."

She followed behind him, knowing she was still bound by the bargain. But she would never promise the other.

When they reached her car, she said, "I'm not leaving my car this time."

"I suppose I can trust you to drive it home," he said.

"I will be there," she said forcefully, reaching in her sweatsuit jacket pocket for her keys.

The pocket was empty.

"Damn!" she muttered.

Miles asked the obvious. "What's wrong?"

"I lost my keys."

"Lost your keys? Where?"

She smiled sweetly. "If I knew that, they wouldn't be lost, now would they?"

"Then you'll have to leave your car and come home with me—"

"No!"

"Don't you have a spare key?"

"In my purse. In the car, under the front seat."

"What's it doing in the car?"

She glared at him. "Does James Bond take a purse on a mission? Does Mother Teresa?"

"Yes, she does," Miles said, trying the driver's door. "I've seen her with one when she comes to raise money in the States."

"Well, Earth Angel leaves hers nice and safe in

the car. See?" She pointed in the passenger window to the front seat. "Nice and safe."

In spite of her standing there, he walked around the car and tried the passenger door. It was locked too. Catherine just shook her head. Miles was from the I-have-to-touch-it-to-believe-it school of thought.

Believing it, he looked at her. "Don't you have one of those little magnetic boxes with the key inside attached under the hood somewhere, just in case you lock your keys in the car?"

"No, because I keep a spare in my wallet just in case I lock my keys in the car."

"Catherine . . ." He took a deep breath. "You'll have to come home with me."

"No, I am not leaving my car again. They must have dropped out of my pocket when I was digging. I'll go back and check."

"It's too danger—"

"Don't be silly," she interrupted, starting off toward the sign. "They're on a glow-in-the-dark key chain, so it'll only take a minute to spot them. Besides, nothing happened when we were putting up the sign. And you can hear me scream. In the meantime, you stay put and watch my car, okay?"

She disappeared into the trees, completely ignoring his protests.

Miles watched her go and debated whether to follow her, then decided not to. She was right; he could hear her easily. Also, she would know exactly where she'd been standing or kneeling, so she had a better chance of finding her keys than he did. And someone really ought to look after the car. Both cars. He prayed the 'Vette was still safe and sound behind the bushes down the road. He could see the bushes, but not the car. He hoped nobody else could see the car, either.

If only he could get in the car, then he could reach the spare keys and they could get out of there. He tried the door again with no luck, then felt for any space around the window edge. It was pressed too tight against the door frame for him to force it down.

He walked around the car and tried the driver's-side window. This one wasn't butted tight against the frame under the rubber gaskets. Still, he couldn't get his fingers in the crack enough to push the window down. The pop-up lock looked promising, though. If he had a hanger, he could feed it through the window and maybe get the lock up.

He looked around and realized there was enough trash along the road's shoulder to provide a hanger . . . or something close.

"I pay good taxes for *this*?" he muttered as he surveyed the litter. "Aha!"

He picked up a thin loop of metal that had caught his eye. It was rusted but still flexible. He only hoped it was long enough.

At the car he was able to feed it through the window, and he grinned. Pulling it out, he bent a small loop at the end, then fed it back through the opening and began to fish for the lock. A car suddenly swung up behind Catherine's, its head-lights shining right on him. The bubble lights on the roof weren't swirling red, but Miles still got a queasy feeling in the pit of his stomach. Two policemen got out of the car.

"Good evening, officers," Miles said cheerfully. "I'm afraid I locked myself out of the car."

"May I see your license and registration?" one asked.

He casually dropped the wire and got out his wallet. "I just have my license. My registration is in the car."

"Thank you," the officer said as he took it. He headed back to the squad car. The other officer pulled out the wire.

Miles smiled and shrugged. The cop didn't. He wondered what the hell was keeping Catherine.

About a minute later, the first officer returned. "This car is registered to a Catherine Wagner. Would you step over to the squad car, sir?"

"But—"

"Step over to the car, sir," the other cop said, taking out his handcuffs.

Miles stared at them, shocked. "What are you doing?"

"Taking you in. Will you step over to the car now, sir?"

"No, I will not," Miles began.

The cop grabbed his arm and snapped a cuff on his wrist. "I'm afraid you are now resisting arrest. You have the right to remain silent . . ."

Miles started to open his mouth to tell them about Catherine being in the deserted lot. He kept it shut, though, when he realized the officers would discover Earth Angel. They would both be arrested then. He swore under his breath. Never, never, *never* would he follow her again. He'd retire to a monastery where there was no Catherine to make him physically and emotionally crazy.

And when he got out of the slammer in ten to twelve, he'd kill her.

As she hunkered down among the trees, Catherine clamped her hands over her mouth to silence her laughter as she watched Philadelphia's premier banker get arrested. She shouldn't be laughing. She knew she really shouldn't. But the look on Miles's face . . .

By the time the police car rolled away, tears were streaming down her face. She was still snickering and wiping at her tears when she finally emerged from her hiding place, her keys safe in her pocket.

She supposed she ought to go bail him out.

The thought had her laughing all over again.

Seven

"Kitteridge?"

"Here!" Miles pushed himself away from the wall.

"Someone made your bail."

"About time." He walked over to the cell door, then turned and waved to Iggy and Righteous William, who were in for robbing a convenience store. "I'm sprung, fellas. It's been a pleasure."

Iggy pushed his wavy blond hair from his eyes. "See ya 'round, dude."

Righteous William gave him the victory fist. He had yet to speak. With his staring eyes and "Mother Doom" tattoo on his shoulder, the man was scary enough without words.

The sound of the lock opening was sweet to Miles. Standing on the other side of the bars was even sweeter. But the greatest pleasure was yet to come—when he had his hands around Catherine's throat. He would kill her for this. And he *still* didn't know what that sign said.

His morale rose 200 percent as he walked out of the cell-block area in the precinct station. He was shocked to see daylight through the grimy windows. It had seemed an eternity since they'd put him in the holding cell, and now he realized it was. As he'd waited impatiently for someone to arrive and straighten out the mix-up, he'd had time to think. He couldn't get the image of those rusting drums leaking toxic chemicals out of his mind. He didn't like what he'd seen, and knew something had to be done.

Catherine and his grandmother were sitting on a bench on the far side of the lobby. Catherine was still dressed in jeans and sweatjacket, her auburn hair falling around her shoulders. She looked like a teenager. The moment she spotted him, she broke into giggles.

"Wait until I get you out of here," he muttered as she approached him.

She actually leaned against him and giggled even more. "Don't make me laugh. My sides are already hurting. Besides, who do you think explained what happened and bailed you out?"

"*Who* had the money to bail him out?" Lettice asked, joining them.

"You," Catherine said. "But I got him off."

He looked down at her, acutely aware of how grimy, bleary-eyed, and unshaven he was. "I am eternally grateful," he said dryly.

"Now who's being prickly?" She glanced up at him, then wrapped her arms around him and burst into laughter.

The feel of her body snuggled against his dissolved his hours of anger. Killing her didn't seem to be as satisfactory an idea as it had been. There were others ways to wreak his vengeance. He patted her on the back and resigned himself to being the brunt of a great joke—for the moment.

"Miles, you have damaged the family honor beyond repair," Lettice said. She was smiling, though, an occasional snort of amusement escaping her lips. "You're nearly as bad as your cousin Rick. I love it."

"Rick?" He frowned in puzzlement. "Rick's the upright English gentleman. He's never done anything bad in his life."

His grandmother leaned closer. "Except rob a robber's house. My grandchildren are turning out to be quite a surprise."

The sergeant beckoned Miles over before he could ask more. He unwrapped Catherine and collected his things. The sergeant was much more courteous this time than he had been the night before.

Out in the sunshine again, he breathed a sigh of relief to be away from the smells and the tension. It had been a long night. Which reminded him . . .

"Where the hell were you?" he asked Catherine. "I was in there all night!"

"Making bail," she said, giggling again. "It took us a while to find out which precinct you were in—"

"Where were you when they were arresting me?" he interrupted.

"Yes," Lettice broke in. "Where were the two of you when they were arresting you?"

"On a mission," Catherine said. "Miles, I was going to come out of the trees—"

"Trees?" Lettice's eyes widened. "What were you doing in trees?"

"Hiding," Miles said. Then he remembered a vital point. "My car! Where's my car?"

"I got your housekeeper's husband to pick it up," Catherine answered. "He must be wondering about all these cars in strange places."

Miles relaxed.

His grandmother didn't. "What cars? What strange places?"

He ignored her. So did Catherine, as she continued, "And the reason I didn't pop up and say, 'Over here, boys,' is because that would have given everything away. Why didn't you tell them about me? You wouldn't have been arrested then."

"Given what away?" Lettice asked. "What are you two talking about?"

"You know and I know we would have been arrested for worse," Miles muttered. Okay, he thought, so he preferred to be arrested for grand theft auto rather than be convicted as a pollution commando, but that didn't mean he was letting her off the hook.

"See?" Catherine said, nodding in satisfaction. "I knew that, so what are you complaining about?"

"Wait a minute!" Lettice explained. "What are you two talking about, you could have been arrested for worse? What about the cars in strange places? What did you two *do* last night?"

"We put up a sign," Catherine said.

Miles shot her a dour look. Taking her arm, he dragged her down the few steps to the sidewalk. Her perfume teased his senses, and reminded him that he was covered in jail grunge. "We're going home. I need a bath and a shave and a nap and a chain for you. Not necessarily in that order."

Catherine erupted into laughter again.

"What do you mean by a chain for Catherine?" Lettice asked, following them. "*What* were you two doing last night in the trees? Miles, answer me!"

"I can't give you anything but love, baby," he sang in reply, feeling like a bewildered Cary Grant tangling with a dizzy heiress, a screwy grandmother, and a full-grown man-eating leopard.

The leopard sounded the easiest of the lot.

"So how was it?" Catherine asked, leaning against Miles's bedroom door. He was dressed in pajama bottoms, and she watched him concentrate on putting on his watch. She knew it was dangerous to be there, but after her shower she had seen his open door and couldn't resist teasing him about his unfortunate incarceration.

"Aggravating," he answered. "Iggy and Righteous William weren't so bad, though."

"Iggy and Righteous William?" she echoed, but her mind wasn't on the conversation. Instead, she was noticing how his biceps bulged slightly. His chest and shoulders were well defined, and his stomach was flat. It was obvious he worked out on a regular basis. Silky dark chest hair arrowed down his flesh, its destination more intriguing than she cared to admit. The pajama bottoms clung to his hips like a second skin. She pulled the collar of her thick terry robe closer around her neck.

"They were my cell mates," he said, grinning.

"They sound lovely," she said, and laughed as the image of an Iggy and Righteous William locked up with Miles momentarily overrode her fascination with his body.

"Are you going to laugh all day?" he asked, although he didn't sound nearly as irritated as he had two hours ago.

"Probably," she admitted. "Your face when the cops arrested you was priceless. You should have seen it."

"I'm sure you'll remind me of it often," he murmured, walking toward her.

"I promise." She swiped at her tears. "Lordy, what a night."

"You've got to admit I'm a fun guy."

"The best, Miles, the best."

"Just so you know it." He touched her arm. "Catherine, I have only one question."

She straightened at his serious tone. "What?"

"What did the sign say?"

That did it. She collapsed against him and roared with laughter. He put his arms around her, literally holding her up. His chest hairs tickled her nose. She tried to regain her composure, but the laughter kept breaking out. The memory of Miles being cuffed and hauled away would stay with her forever.

He sighed. "I hope you're still laughing when this gets in the papers. Because I'll kill you then."

"Oh, come on, Miles," she said, lifting her head. "It was all a mix-up, and I've already straightened it out. It's never going to get into the papers. Although . . ." The giggles started once more at the thought of blaring *Philadelphia Inquirer* headlines. That would just about make up for the mess he'd once made of her life.

"That's right, laugh." He patted her back. "Get it all out so I can shoot you and hang you and draw and quarter you—"

"It'd be worth it!" she gasped. "Oh, Miles."

"Say my name like that, and I'll follow you anywhere."

He tilted her head back so her gaze could meet his. The amusement and camaraderie quickly changed to something else. The sharp clean scent of soap and male invaded her nostrils. Thick heat began to flow inside her, and she unwittingly stroked his warm skin. "Miles . . ."

Suddenly, he was more dangerous than ever. Even as she realized it, his mouth descended on hers, his tongue thrusting through her astonished gasp.

The invasion was unexpected, bringing surprise and confusion. She knew she should be fighting to get away, but her insides were melting at the taste of him on her lips. Whatever was wrong with Miles, this was right.

Common sense still valiantly rose up in her. She managed to tear her mouth from his. She was panting for breath. "Miles. We have an agreement—"

"You broke it last night." His eyes were gleaming with satisfaction.

"I did not!" she exclaimed. "I told you I was coming back."

"All bets are off, Catherine." He strung kisses along her jaw, just under her ear. Sweet, light kisses that were designed to confuse her.

They were doing a good job of it, she admitted, trying to keep from pressing herself to him. "I'll escape."

"I've got my tie . . ." He pulled her closer, his mouth nibbling at her throat in a way that released a flood of desire in her body.

"The shutoff valves will probably . . . be discovered today." That she had given away the mission didn't matter. She had to stop the seduction before she succumbed.

"How nice." His lips grazed hers. Once. Twice. His breath fanned her cheek. "Ah, Catherine . . ."

"The agreement's done, anyway," she said in a last effort to control her wayward emotions. His skin was hot under her fingers, spurring an even greater heat within her. If only he hadn't made her laugh. Anger kept the armor in place, but laughter opened the gates.

He pushed the door shut behind her. "Then let's make a new agreement."

His mouth settled firmly on hers, and she was undone. Her hands crept up around his shoulders, exploring the hard muscles and bone. Her tongue dueled with his. Everything about him was overwhelming her senses, and she could remember how close she had come to throwing away fiancé and marriage to be in his arms like this. An obtuse little voice told her she should have. . . .

His hands slid down her back, then pulled her against him. She groaned into his mouth as everything inside her went wild. He excited her in a way she hadn't thought was possible. Miles Kitteridge was the one man who could shatter her control and throw her equilibrium right out the window. Under his suave exterior, he was the bad boy, the man all sensible women ran from, the one who kept them on a string. She felt the challenge to try to change the bad boy, to see if she was the one who could conquer him. She knew he would never love her, but to have the closeness just once, to claim him . . . just once . . .

His hands slipped under her robe, and her

flimsy nightgown was no barrier. He had her wrapped so tightly against him, she couldn't breathe and she didn't care. His palm grazed her breast, sending electric shock waves to her every nerve ending. Then he cupped her fully, his thumb brushing back and forth across her nipple. She thought she would explode from the sensation.

"Catherine." His voice was raspy, and it sent shivers of heat down her spine. His hands were leading her to the bed. She couldn't have stopped herself if she'd wanted to. And she didn't. It seemed as if she'd wanted this forever.

He stared down at her, almost willing her to stop him as he slipped the robe from her shoulders. It fell in a puddle at her feet. He reached out and traced a finger along her collarbone, down around the curve of her breast, her nipple. Her eyelids fluttered closed, and she took a deep breath against the sensual waves rocking her. She opened her eyes and touched him in wonder, letting her hand wander across his chest, pausing to delight in the hard muscles and the tangle of chest hair. He sucked in his breath, then her nightgown joined her robe. His mouth covered hers in a devastating kiss.

Catherine clawed and whimpered at the raw passion that leaped between them. It was too overwhelming and too honest to deny. She fell onto the bed, pulling him on top of her, taking his weight with a deep satisfaction. The feel of flesh to flesh snatched her breath away. He fit her perfectly, and her hips made a natural cradle for his.

His kisses were everywhere, tasting, nibbling, branding. She arched herself into his mouth, the delicious feel of his tongue bringing her nipples to hard points. She ached for him, realizing now that her verbal sparring with him was only a cover for the passion he ignited in her. Her response to him shook her to the core. But there was more, so much more, that her closeness to him the last few days had brought to the surface. The barrier she had guarded so carefully and had finally let down was not a trap.

Miles knew what little control he had was slipping away as Catherine writhed beneath him. Never had he found such breathtaking passion in a woman. Her hands ignited fires inside him that flowed along his veins like heated wine. He had waited for this—waited years for the slow fire to consume him. Every move she made challenged him, enticed him. He would never possess her. She would possess him. Her hands caressed his back, sliding down his skin, then nearly driving him over the edge as they dipped under the waistband of his pajama bottoms. He reached between them, spanning his hand across her abdomen. She cried out his name and dug her fingers into his hips when his hand slipped lower to find her woman's flesh tight and hot. His control broke with a vengeance. He kicked his pajamas off, then lifted his body over hers and united himself with her.

"Sweet Lord, Catherine." He gasped for air. All his fantasies had never even come close to the reality of her.

"Miles, please. I want you very much."

They moved together in the ultimate gift of man and woman. With every thrust they gave and took in a wondrous exchange. Passion was overcome by need . . . and more. Catherine arched herself up to him as the sweet oblivion finally overtook her, and Miles plunged after her, the culmination swift and intense, until there was nothing left in the storm but each other.

Catherine slowly rose to the light again, growing aware of Miles on her, naked and contented. No man had ever claimed her as he had. No man could break her as he could. Too late, she thought in despair as every barrier she possessed snapped back into place. Too late.

She knew she had been a fool to think she could steal this one time with him and walk away. Somehow, despite everything she knew about him, every shred of common sense she had, she had fallen in love with him.

"I do believe we've reached a new agreement," he murmured, nuzzling her throat.

Disappointment shot through her. But what had she expected to hear? she asked herself. His undying love? "Miles, this was a mistake."

He raised his head. "Catherine, I've made a lot of mistakes in my life, but this isn't one of them, trust me."

That was the point, she thought. She *couldn't* trust him with her heart.

"Now don't get all prickly on me after I got arrested for you," he said, kissing her under her earlobe.

She squirmed at the erotic sensation tingling her flesh.

He spread kisses down her neck. "Catherine, be soft for once . . . for now."

She closed her eyes. It was a request she couldn't deny him, for the moment. But she would have to correct things later with cold, calculating Miles, if only for her sanity's sake.

She wondered which would break her more—being with Miles, or being without him.

The telephone blaring in his ear brought Miles out of a dead sleep.

He jumped in shock, disoriented, then scrambled up and snatched the receiver.

"Hello," he said, realizing at the same moment that Catherine was no longer in the bed with him.

"Miles! You're there! I've called everywhere for you."

Byrne Wagner's voice was a bellow. Miles winced, the lack of sleep making him feel as if he had a hangover.

"I have to go, Byrne," he said, beginning to put down the phone.

"That damn Earth Angel manually turned off the pumping system at the refinery!" Byrne screeched into the telephone. "Everyone was looking for a breakdown and the valves were shut! Meeting as soon as you can get here. This time we're going to stop that—that—"

"Has Catherine been called?" Miles interrupted.

A long pause ensued. "Her house was called," Byrne said finally. "She wasn't home."

"Are you going to track her down like you did me?"

"What the hell are all these questions for? She'll be called." Byrne slammed down the telephone.

Miles set his down more thoughtfully. Something would have to be done about Byrne, and quickly. He had some ideas about that, but right

now he had to find his wandering angel. He
scowled at the thought that she could make love
with him and leave immediately after. The sun was
low in the sky, indicating it was late afternoon.
Who knew how long she had been gone. Byrne and
his damn meeting could wait.

He threw on trousers and a shirt, and grabbed a
jacket and tie as he half-ran out of the bedroom. He
strode quickly down the hall, past Sheba's room,
then tracked back when something caught his eye.

Catherine had her small weekender on the bed
and was calmly packing her clothes into it. Sheba
was lying at the foot of the bed, her plumed tail
twitching in annoyance.

Catherine glanced at him, then went back to her
packing.

"Get out your power suit," he said, choosing to
ignore the bag and her retreat from his bedroom.
"Byrne's just called another emergency meeting."

She smiled a tiny smile of amusement and set
down the shirt she was holding. "For which disaster? The shutdown or the sign?"

"The shutdown. I don't think they've found the
sign yet."

"They will. Earth Angel called the TV stations
about an hour ago."

"You've been up for a while," he commented,
walking into the room. He sat down on the bed and
stroked Sheba. The cat purred, unconcerned with
the awkwardness between the humans.

Catherine turned to look at him. "The agreement's over, Miles. I'm going home."

"I can't allow that. You'll be doing more Earth
Angel things."

"What will you do? Keep a chain on me?"

He grinned. "Now that has distinct possibili—"

"And after I bailed you out?" The words were light, but her tone wasn't.

He reached for her. "Catherine . . ."

She backed away. "What happened was a mistake, Miles. You know it and I know it."

"It seemed pretty perfect to me," he said, staring at her. This wasn't the aftermath to their lovemaking that he'd been expecting.

She shook her head. "Look, it would never work, so let's not belabor the point."

"There's more to this than a difference of philosophies—"

"Miles, I'm determined to expose what's been going on, and you're determined to stop me—"

"Because I don't want you hurt! And because there are other ways of doing—"

"No, there aren't."

"Yes, there are."

"Miles, what are you looking for in a relationship with me?"

"I . . ." He hesitated, knowing she wanted answers he wasn't ready to give. "I care. I can't answer anything more beyond that."

"I see."

He felt oddly defeated. Rising to his feet, he said, "Get dressed, Catherine. We've got a meeting to go to."

"I'm not staying here, Miles."

"Get dressed," he repeated, and stalked out of the room.

Her uncle looked more livid than ever, Catherine thought as she took a seat at the conference table as far away from Miles as she could get. It seemed like a dream that she had been in his bed that morning, making love. What was all too real was his lack of an answer to her question.

Risking a glance at him, she saw he didn't look much better than Byrne. She had the impression the two men were angry with each other, but that notion was ludicrous.

Byrne launched into a tirade on the shutdown valves. Catherine schooled her features into a poker expression. Her aunt Sylvia was sitting next to her, and she had the strangest idea Sylvia was amused by Earth Angel's latest antics.

"I'm ordering the guards to shoot anyone on sight!" Byrne exclaimed, slamming his hand on the table.

Catherine stiffened. Miles raised his eyebrow at her, clearly telling her he'd predicted this.

"Don't act sillier than you already are," Sylvia said. "We'd be up for murder charges. I suggest that we hire more security, have constant checks of the perimeter and all outbuildings, and update the system, as Father proposed. This would never have happened if we hadn't been so cheap in the first place—"

"We don't need all that," Byrne said, gazing around the room, a smirk on his face. "I've received some information . . ."

Catherine suddenly had a bad feeling about that information.

". . . that someone has been illegally dumping drums of waste products on a lot at this end of the city, and has put up a sign accusing us of doing it. Well, we have *not* been doing it, but in a magnan-

EARTH ANGEL • 125

imous gesture I ordered a complete cleanup of the lot."

Heads nodded sagely. Catherine barely restrained a snort of disgust.

"I have been investigating who the Earth Angel is," Byrne continued. The smirk widened. "And finally, I have some evidence that proves beyond a shadow of a doubt who this criminal is."

Catherine didn't move. Her heart thumped painfully.

"Shocking evidence," Byrne continued.

Catherine braced herself.

"The Earth Angel is . . ." Byrne dramatically pointed his finger at the culprit. "Miles."

Eight

Catherine erupted into laughter.

Miles grimaced at her, fighting the urge to either strangle her or kiss her. Both appealed, as usual. But she was lessening the tension in the room. He could see the others visibly relaxing.

"I'm sorry," Catherine gasped in between fits of giggles. "It's just that . . . Miles of all people. That's a good one, Uncle Byrne."

"I have information!" Byrne bellowed at her.

Catherine roared.

Miles sat back in his chair and eyed Byrne for a long moment. If there was one thing he knew, it was how not to react. He also knew how to relax in the heat of a crisis. Finally, he said, "Your 'information' is nonsense, Byrne."

"Right before this meeting began," Byrne said, "a reporter got through and confronted me about a police report that you were at that lot last night. What were you doing there, Miles, if you're *not* the Earth Angel?"

So much for the record being expunged, Miles

thought. Clearly, the wheels of justice ground slowly. He scratched his chin and said the only thing he could think to say. "I had a tip the Earth Angel would be there, and I went to catch him."

Byrne gaped at him. "But . . . but . . ."

"Catherine can confirm it. She was with me," Miles added, deciding to stave off any further revelations. If Byrne had found this much out, he'd eventually uncover whose car was involved. "What I'd like to talk about are the leaking drums buried there—"

"Why didn't you and Catherine catch the Angel?" Catherine's father asked, obviously curious.

Miles stared at him, his mind scrambling for an answer to the unexpected question.

"You had a tip," Gerald continued. "You were staking out the field. How could that sign go up without your seeing who did it?"

"Dad, we were . . ." Catherine looked at Miles in a panic.

"Busy," he finished helplessly.

"Busy!" Byrne exclaimed. "Busy!"

"Busy, Byrne," Sylvia said, grinning. "Like you're busy with that woman up in Ardmore three nights a week—"

"Sylvia!"

But everyone was laughing and smiling knowing smiles. The implication Sylvia had made was clear to everyone. Catherine's face was bright red. Miles had no doubt she was furious and embarrassed— especially knowing Sylvia had hit the mark. He shrugged. He wasn't about to confess their real purpose, and he doubted Catherine would, either. She was smart enough to realize that if she did, the entire family would swing back to Byrne. Besides, her Earth Angel activities would have to come to an end. He doubted she was ready for that.

But Byrne, on the other hand, would *have* to be stopped.

"Well, this is wonderful," Gerald said. "She's finally showing some sense in her choice of men."

The insensitive words were like a slap, and Miles gritted his teeth to hold his temper. This was her father, after all, so it wouldn't do to punch his lights out. No wonder Catherine kept a lot of emotional doors closed. He looked directly at her and smiled to ease the hurt her father must have caused. "I'm the one who's showing some sense. I consider myself lucky that Catherine doesn't run for the hills."

She frowned, as if puzzled by his words. The funny thing was, he meant them. He reminded himself of the packed bag at his house. He couldn't let her go, not after the way they'd made love, not after the way she'd possessed him. He could still feel her . . . feel the way they had moved together . . . feel the shudder of spent passion rush through him fast and furious.

"People," Catherine said, "you all are acting as if this is something permanent. Miles and I just had a . . . date to catch the Angel. I got the tip too."

"You two are perfectly matched," Sylvia said, disregarding her niece's words. "I've always thought so."

"Can we stop playing *Hello, Dolly* and get back to the meeting at hand?" Byrne asked in a loud voice. "I would like to know why Miles and Catherine did not see fit to tell anyone—like our security people or the police—about this tip."

"Welll . . ." Miles felt like he was doing a Ronald Reagan imitation.

"There wasn't time," Catherine broke in, before he could finish. "We got the tip so late. Besides, it could have been a crank, and wouldn't Miles and I have looked silly if we were wrong?"

"Makes perfect sense to me," Sylvia said.

The others nodded. Miles realized that with a little coaching to keep her temper in place, Catherine could sway her relatives into anything. That gave him an idea, a brilliant idea, on how to stop Byrne and keep Catherine with him.

"It doesn't make sense to me," Byrne muttered, and took another swig of Maalox. "If the two lovebirds get another 'tip,' I suggest they stop playing Nick and Nora Charles and pass it along to someone who can do some good with it."

"Of course," Miles said, grinning at the turn of events.

"Besides," Sylvia teased, "you two might just forget yourselves again under the moonlit sky."

Catherine smiled thinly. "Thank you, Aunt Sylvia. I do believe we're at an emergency meeting . . ."

Everyone straightened and became serious again. Miles raised his eyebrows. His theory had more possibilities by the second.

The meeting lasted about fifteen more minutes, with no solution except to do as Sylvia suggested and beef up the security and update the system. The relatives supported it, in spite of Byrne's protests about the expense. They also decided to be bold, for once, and host a big media reception as soon as possible. Byrne nearly popped his suspenders at that one.

When the meeting broke up, Catherine made her usual exit, with a flare of skirt across her delicious legs. Damn, but she did it better than anyone else, Miles thought happily.

Unfortunately, it also signaled that she was furious.

He sighed and hurried to catch up with her.

Catherine strode toward the elevator, her annoyance pounding harder with each step.

She couldn't believe the conclusions her relatives had reached in there concerning her and Miles. *And he'd allowed it!* Her face heated painfully when she thought of the teasing and the way they'd all grinned at her like amorous jackasses.

"Catherine."

The voice behind her was all too distinctive. She'd heard it whisper her name in the heat of passion. And that was all it had been. Passion. She kept walking.

"Catherine!" He caught up with her in a few quick strides.

"Go away." Her self-righteous anger weakened with him so close to her. She could feel him again . . . the way they'd moved together . . . the way she'd clawed and cried out his name. She wished she had never given in to the fantasy.

"Come on, Catherine," he said, amusement heavy in his voice. "It was just a mistake."

She whirled to face him. "And you *let* them make it!"

"What was I supposed to do? Tell the truth?"

"That would be nice for a change."

"I'd be more impressed with that if *you* hadn't been Silent Sal."

She set her jaw, knowing she couldn't explain why she hadn't confessed. It had been the prime opportunity to humiliate her family with the revelation that Earth Angel was among them, yet it had seemed a childish reaction to past hurts. Besides, the tide was turning against Byrne, and she sensed she would have put everyone firmly back in his camp if she'd confessed. Still, she was not about to answer Miles.

"Silent Sal again," he said.

"You don't have to be so damned smug," she muttered as they reached the express elevator between the conference floor and the first floor lobby. She jabbed the down button.

"I'm entitled," he said, "I did like Byrne's comment about Nick and Nora Charles. I'm surprised he knew who they were."

"Only from the movies," she said. "You don't think he's actually read any Hammett, do you?"

"Good point."

When they were alone in the elevator, Miles said casually, "The police aren't speed demons."

"The report probably hadn't been removed yet." She shrugged. "It was bad timing."

"Let's make sure that's the only bad timing. Catherine, no more Earth Angel antics. It's going to be too risky now—"

"This elevator could be bugged," she reminded him.

He snorted. "I wouldn't put much past Byrne, but that's too farfetched even for him. Catherine, promise me."

She glanced at him, then back at the doors. "I thought my promise wasn't worth anything."

"Catherine . . ." He changed his tone. "What if I told you there's a way to eliminate Byrne and get all the changes you want for Wagner Oil."

"Are you going to call a hit man?"

He grinned. "We get the board to remove him as chairman—"

She laughed. "With this crowd? You've got to be kidding."

"Pay attention in there, my friend," he chided. "Byrne is losing ground with every turn. We only have to push him along."

She eyed him narrowly. "Oh, sure. If you actually manage this major miracle, who would take his place that has enough sense to move into the twenty-first century? They all think exactly like him."

"All except one." His grin widened. "You."

She gaped at him, her thoughts all clashing together in complete astonishment and confusion. He couldn't have surprised her more if he'd suggested Ralph Nader for chairman of the board.

The elevator bell dinged.

"Ground floor," Miles announced. "Everybody out."

"You're nuts," Catherine said.

Miles chuckled as he opened the front door to his house. "You've said that all the way home."

"And I'm still saying it, Miles. You're nuts."

"One has to be in dire situations. Look at Earth Angel."

"You're more nuts than me."

She stepped over the threshold without a bit of hesitation, her focus all on his proposed board change. He mentally breathed a sigh of relief. If they hadn't come back together in his car to discuss the meeting, he never would have gotten her this far. Now all he had to do was keep her here.

She swung around. "Miles, I can't run the corporation. I'm only twenty-nine, and I've only been with Wagner for a couple of years."

"We'll get you a solid CEO. There's a million of them out there." He took her hand. She immediately withdrew it. He didn't comment on her gesture, although it hurt more than he cared to admit. "I will state this one more time for the record, Catherine. You are the only one who's even thinking of the future. You know where the business has to go. Byrne is not going to change his attitude. He'll still be trying to widen the profit margin by eliminating 'unnecessary' safety procedures. And as long as he's there, we'll be paying EPA fines until we have no profits at all. Earth Angel isn't going to make a damn bit of difference beyond embarrassing him. If she keeps it up, the rest will eventually become irritated with it and swing back to Byrne. Worse, they'll get used to it, and she won't have the impact she has now. He has to be taken out, or a lot of people who depend on Wagner Oil will suffer. The board's ripe for an ouster."

She gazed at him for a long moment. "He's my uncle."

"He's ruining the company."

"It wouldn't be a board fight. It would be a family fight."

"It's what you've been doing all this time," he said. "Didn't you realize it would come to this if Earth Angel was successful?"

"I never set out to oust anyone," she said hotly. "I just wanted to get them to do the right thing about the Utah land—"

"Then you were naive if you thought Byrne would come over to your way of thinking. The man isn't capable. You know in your heart I'm right about this."

"I don't know anything!" she exclaimed.

But Miles knew she could see the sense of it. She was shaking with the knowledge. He wanted to reach out and hold her, but she probably wouldn't accept him.

"How can you stand there and ask me to destroy my family?" she said, her voice catching. "How can you turn it off like that?"

He smiled gently. "There are always going to be hard decisions that are the best decisions, Catherine. And usually the right one is the hardest of all to make. But the sooner you do it, the less pain there'll be. This is the only way to save Wagner Oil. The situation's perfect now. It's business, and your family will understand that."

"Gee, but you're wonderfully cynical. I can't be like you, Miles. I can't grab the brass ring just because it's there."

"If you want to stop the pollution, you will."

"The codicil will stop them when it's found."

He shook his head. "We haven't found it yet. You may be banking a little too much on the family's blindly following it, anyhow. What about the next crisis with Byrne? The codicil won't cover that one. My way is a permanent solution to the problem."

"I'm going," she said, turning toward the stairs.

His stomach twisted. "Can't we talk about this?"

"There's nothing to talk about."

"Catherine." Her name was a plea. "Don't go."

"I'm not staying, Miles." She climbed the stairs. "There's nothing to stay for."

Miles strode into his study. He poured himself a Scotch, neat, and drank it down in one gulp.

Let her go, he told himself. She didn't budge an inch anywhere, and he was damned tired of being the villain in her book. What the hell did she want from him, anyway? The last time he'd made a commitment, it had been a disaster. Couldn't she give them both time to get used to their relationship? Why the hell did she have to rush in like a firebomb and demand more than he was ready for? Why couldn't she just stay and explore what they had?

He wouldn't beg, he decided as he heard the front door slam shut. He would not beg.

Twenty seconds later, he found himself out in front of her car. Begging.

"Catherine, please don't go." He squeezed himself between her and the driver's door.

She faced him squarely. "I can't do what you want, Miles. It makes me sick to think of it."

"I'm not some ogre, you know."

She smiled sadly. "Everything is business to you. Everything. Even your cat."

"What the hell does Sheba have to do with anything?"

"You don't even see it, do you?" She shook her head. "We don't think alike. You'll never want what I want."

He pulled her to him. His fingers traced her cheek. "Doesn't this count for anything?"

She took a deep shuddering breath. "It isn't enough."

"It's everything," he murmured, burying his face in her silky hair.

She rested her forehead against his shoulder. "Let me go, Miles."

Pain knifed through him. He tightened his fingers around her arms for one long moment . . . then dropped his hands away.

He set his jaw as she got into the little car. The engine kicked over instantly. She put the car in gear and drove down the driveway without once looking back.

"Damn you, Catherine," he whispered, as he watched the taillights disappear around the bend.

He felt as if he had lost his heart.

"My grandson is miserable."

Catherine sighed as she looked at Lettice, sitting across the table from her. "You didn't ask me to lunch at Chef Tell's just to tell me that, surely."

Lettice ignored the redirection. "I still want to know what happened. First he's sending you cure-alls by the pound and getting himself arrested to your great amusement—which neither of you has yet explained, by the way. But now he's colder than a witch's . . . He's worse. I have seen my children and grandchildren in pain before, but I have never seen any of them like this. He's an emotional zombie. And you don't look much better."

She didn't want to hear this, Catherine thought. She knew she shouldn't have come. But Lettice had been so insistent, and she hadn't been able to resist hearing some tidbit about Miles. "Lettice, Miles has always been cold."

"Not lately. Lately, he's been hot as the tropics. And don't try feeding me some line about how there's nothing between you two. I'm not blind, and I'm not a fool."

Catherine shrugged as casually as she could. She had to remain cool or else the misery she'd endured the past three days would erupt again.

"Catherine."

The prompt was all too reminiscent of Miles's. She swallowed back a rush of emotion. "What he wants I can't give. What I want he can't give."

"That's no answer."

"That's all you're going to get."

Leaning forward in her chair, Lettice eyed her. Catherine resisted the urge to babble the truth. How did the lady provoke that sensation with one look?

"That's no answer, either," Lettice said. "But I suppose I won't get one anyway. You evaded me pretty well when we had to bail Miles out of prison."

Catherine actually chuckled. "It was only a holding cell."

"Whatever. And that was no power breakfast that morning. A grandmother knows."

Catherine's smile turned to a grimace. She thought her head would explode from all the probing. Why couldn't Lettice leave it alone?

"Well, far be it from me to poke my nose in where it doesn't belong," Lettice announced, sitting back in her chair.

"And I'm Barbara Bush," Catherine muttered.

"I'm restraining myself, so don't blow it."

Catherine clamped her lips shut over a retort.

"You two are all grown up now, so you can ruin your lives if you want. Far be it from me to try to stop you and Miles from the stupidest mistake of your lives."

Lettice was a real confidence builder, Catherine thought. She buttered her roll with vigor.

"I suppose I should get to the reason for lunch," Lettice continued. "I . . . Actually I haven't quite figured out a way to tell you this." Her hesitant tone sent shivers of dread along Catherine's spine. "It's about your grandfather's codicil."

"You *still* can't remember the lawyers he used for that," Catherine guessed, her heart sinking.

"Catherine." Lettice reached out and took her hand. "I'm an old woman. I don't see and hear things as well as I used to."

"What are you saying?"

"That I think now I must have been mistaken about a codicil." Lettice's voice was gentle, but that didn't stop the shock.

"Mistaken?" Catherine echoed blankly.

The older woman nodded. "I'm afraid so. I have tried so hard to remember the lawyer, and I finally realized the reason I can't is because there might not have been one. I'm so sorry, Catherine, but I think I might have mixed things up."

"Mixed things up?" Catherine asked, her heart thumping painfully. "Are you saying there isn't a codicil?"

"I'm not sure what I saw. I had thought it was an addition to his will, but now I'm not so sure. It's all muddled up in my mind. I know he talked about a codicil. Maybe that's what I'm confusing."

Catherine shook her head to deny the words. "But, Lettice, all this time—"

Lettice patted her hand. "I'm very sorry. You'll have to find some other way to save the land."

"There is no other way."

"Of course there is." Lettice raised her eyebrows. "Catherine, there always is another way for anything in life. Now quit feeling sorry for yourself and get out there and do it."

"That's a great pep rally you give," Catherine muttered.

Catherine watched the antacid tablets fizz in the squat glass of water. She threw a couple of ice cubes in to chill it, then swallowed the liquid. It would be a miracle, though, if the stuff managed to get rid of the raging headache and flipping stomach she'd acquired at lunch.

She turned around in her office chair and stared out the window, blindly watching the activity at the refinery plant. How could Lettice have gotten things so confused? And why hadn't she recognized it sooner?

Catherine hated to admit it, but Miles had been right about one thing. She had been depending too much on that codicil. She should have known when it couldn't be traced that it was more than just lost. Her problem was that she had hoped against hope.

She finally acknowledged that her grandfather might not have followed through on the codicil. After all, he hadn't put the land in trust to protect it.

Despite her best efforts to resist it, Miles's solution drifted through her mind like a seductive harem dancer. When he had first suggested it, she had been horrified . . . and tempted. Byrne was ruining Wagner Oil, and someone had to stop him. They were trying to run a multimillion-dollar business, not decide who got to go to the family cabin during the skiing season. But it *would* cause a family rift, and she didn't want to be instrumental in that. As an officer of the corporation, she also had an obligation to do what was right for the corporation and its employees.

She *had* been naive about where the Earth Angel exploits would lead. Looking back, she could see they would lead nowhere else. What Miles proposed was right. And it was time she took responsibility for her actions.

Catherine closed her eyes for a long moment, then opened them. Screwing up her courage, she swiveled around in her chair, picked up the telephone, and dialed Miles's number.

His secretary answered after the third ring. Catherine identified herself.

"Yes, Miss Wagner. I'll put him right on."

She didn't even have time to blink, let alone hang up, before Miles was on the line.

"Catherine."

Her heart leaped and her blood pounded at the way he said her name. She forced the sensations away. "Hello, Miles."

"You haven't returned any of my calls. There were more than two this time."

She hadn't returned them because there was no sense in torturing herself. "Miles, do you remember the problem we discussed the other day?"

There was a long pause. "Yes, I remember."

His voice sounded odd, almost as if he were disappointed. She told herself not to be foolish. "I would like to reconsider the option you mentioned."

This time the pause was longer, and when he spoke, his voice was excited. "I'm pleased. Can we meet about this?"

She drew in a deep breath. "Yes."

Nine

Miles grimaced. This wasn't quite what he'd had in mind. He had hoped they would meet in a more intimate setting, not his office. His gleaming walnut desk might as well have been an ocean between them. He was certainly no closer to her than he'd been when she called an hour ago. He really had to cut down on his optimistic streak.

"We didn't have to do this here," he said.

Sitting back in the deep wing chair, Catherine just looked at him. "*My* office was hardly appropriate."

"I meant we could have met in a restaurant."

"Miles, could we just get down to business?"

She wasn't budging an inch, he thought. As usual. Catherine was the most uncompromising woman he'd ever met. And he'd never been more miserable without her. Today she looked . . . defeated. The turquoise suit she wore was modest, yet it outlined her body in a way that sent his pulse racing. He knew what lay underneath. Her auburn hair was pulled back from her face, emphasizing its strong features, yet leaving her vulnerable. His hands itched to reach for her and pull her into his arms. The past three days had been terrible, the nights worse. Everything had blown up in his face, and he didn't know how to fix it. Deciding to take it slow, he said, "I'm surprised you changed your mind."

"Did your grandmother tell you about the codicil?"

He nodded. "I still can't believe she was so mistaken."

"Neither can I."

She shifted in her chair, and the delicious scent of her perfume floated across the room to torture him with remembrances. His blood throbbed in reaction. He wanted to forget the plan and make love. Catherine wouldn't cooperate, though. Dammit.

"I knew Grandmother was getting older," he managed to say, sensing she wouldn't appreciate a sudden lunge across the desk. "But I didn't think she could get things so mixed up. Do you think she could be wrong about being wrong? I'm perfectly willing to keep my guy on it."

Catherine shrugged, as if indifferent. He knew better.

"I suppose it wouldn't hurt," she said. "Although it seems senseless now. I may not believe it, but I can't help feeling that it's true."

"I take it the lack of a codicil is what changed your mind about my plan."

She looked away, then back. "Yes."

"Would you leave a maniac in charge of the Green Earth Society?" he asked, deciding to give her an example she would understand.

She blinked. "No."

"That's what you would be doing with Wagner Oil."

"Miles, I already said I was reconsidering."

"Then stop acting like you're a murderer!"

"I'm not!"

"Okay." With effort, he calmed himself. This arguing was getting both of them nowhere. Working on this together would keep them in constant contact. He ought to be concentrating on the opportunities that would provide. "I've been thinking about this, and we have several advantages at the moment. Byrne has not handled the media well, which has damaged the company. Profits were down by 4 percent this morning. *Four more percent* over last week's slight decrease. Everyone is hot to stop further embarrassment, and they're realizing that won't be accomplished through Byrne. Also, they're beginning to take environmental measures seriously, especially since that's what got them into trouble in the first place. And last, Wagner Oil has a balloon payment due next month on the exploration loan I put together for them."

"How is that an advantage?" Catherine asked, puzzled.

"Because they don't have the money for it. Not all of it, anyway." Miles grinned. "Byrne's going to have to ask the bank consortium for an extension of credit."

"Will the consortium demand the entire payment?"

"I can recommend to them that they make the extension . . . if the company shows that it is turning around its current problems."

She raised her eyebrows. "And you'll tell my relatives they have to clean up their act, or else."

"I will suggest it strongly." He chuckled. "I will also suggest strongly that cleanup begins at home."

"And what do I do in all this?" she asked in a cool voice.

"You continue to be the voice of reason and progress, which I will point out at every turn. I will make it clear that you are my choice for a new chairperson." He added sternly, "And you stay home at night. No risky Earth Angel stunts. If you're caught, everything is ruined."

"You've certainly planned this all out."

"I haven't had anything else to do for the past three days."

She didn't answer.

He sighed. "Catherine, I'll be the bad guy in all of this, not you. Do you understand that?"

She nodded, then looked down at her hands. "It seems so . . . easy."

"Only because the time is right. And it won't be easy, believe me."

She focused her gaze on his desk, clearly needing to think. He sat back and gave her the opportunity, while giving himself the opportunity to drink in the sight of her. He felt parched after the drought of days and nights without her. She sat unmoving. How she could be so still amazed him. She always seemed to bring energy into the room with her. At least she sparked quite a lot of it in him.

The minutes dragged out. He began to worry. Catherine looked up at last.

"What's the extra wastebasket for?" she asked.

He blinked, then grinned broadly. "For recycling my paper. I'm separating my trash according to type. Regular trash in one, paper in the other. I've discovered I have very little regular trash."

"That's nice. But what about the metal and leather wastebasket you're putting them in?"

"It's a rock group?" he asked dubiously.

"It's not recyclable, and it'll be around forever," she answered, shaking her head. "Use grocery bags for your recycled paper. That way the container gets recycled too."

He looked around at the expensive oak paneling, the cherrywood and leather furnishings, the Chinese carpets, and imagined a brown paper bag smack in the midst of it. "I'll use this one forever instead. Have you decided yet?"

She made a face. "I hate this. And not just from a personal viewpoint. There's a lot that could go wrong, and the company will still be vulnerable in some ways." She paused. "But I don't see any alternative."

He smiled, enormously relieved. "Good. Now, we don't have much time, so you better move back in with me—"

She was out of the chair and walking. "No, thank you."

Miles leaped to his feet and ran around the desk, stopping her halfway to the door. "Hold on, Catherine—"

"I will not move back in with you, Miles. If this is part of your grand plan, then no deal."

He took a deep breath. "We're going to have to do a lot of planning. Long hours—"

"Then we'll do it and then go home. Separately,"

she said, smiling sweetly. "And that's all we'll be doing together."

His brows drew together. So much for all those opportunities to be with her. Now what did he do? "You are like a brick wall, you know that?"

"I thought talking to me was like talking to the razor's edge."

"This relationship just started, Catherine. How am I supposed to know where it's going? Let's let it go—"

"That's typical of you, Miles," she broke in. "I still won't be a notch on your belt."

"What the hell makes you think it would ever be like that?" he demanded. "You have always treated me like I just climbed out of the primordial slime, and I never did a damn thing to you."

"You ruined my life!" she exclaimed.

"What!" He stared at her. What was this new nonsense? "When? Tell me when."

"The night of that party." Her breath was coming in pants. "I had to take my bar exams the next day. And because of you, I had the worse scores in the history of the Pennsylvania Bar!"

He gaped at her, completely astonished. "Me! I didn't do anything!"

"You asked me into your bed as if I were a piece of meat," she said, bitterness pervading her voice. "I was engaged, the wedding invitations had gone out. I *had* to pass that bar—"

"I didn't even know you were taking it!"

"And it wouldn't have mattered to you if you did." Her eyes blazed, stinging him with her anger.

"But why did my propositioning you bother you

that much?" Suddenly, the answer came to him. He grinned. She had wanted him even then. Enough to upset her equilibrium.

Her face turned red. "Damn you, Miles. I was humiliated, and you think it's a joke."

"I'm sorry about that, Catherine, but the guy was a jerk—"

"Whether he was or not isn't the point. *You* never gave a damn that I was engaged."

"I wouldn't have given a damn whether you were married, Catherine. That's how much I wanted you then." He leaned close, breathing in her heat and letting it swell through his veins. "I wouldn't give a damn if you were still married. That's how much I want you now."

She stepped back. He had the oddest feeling that he couldn't have hurt her more if he had slapped her.

"And what happens to me when the next woman comes along that you want?" she asked. "You'll go for her with all the morals of an alley cat, just as you did with me."

"Wait a minute!" he said, angry and astounded by her accusations. "It's ridiculous to say I ruined your life over one inci—"

"You miss the point. I can't trust you, Miles, because you go for what you want whenever you want it. You don't even hesitate over conscience. Look at how fast you're going for what you want with Wagner Oil, no matter who it hurts. But I'll say one thing for you. At least you're honest in not wanting to make a commitment. You wouldn't know how to honor it, so you don't even try." She walked to the door, then turned around. "I'll do whatever I have to in order to save the company. But I won't do anything more."

She left his office, leaving him gaping.

Catherine raised her head from her pillow and swiped at her tears. She'd never in her life thought that she would be crying over Miles. She also never thought she'd humiliate herself by telling him exactly how much control he could exert over her.

Well, now he knew. He must think she was a lovesick teenager. And he would be right. It was the final blow to her dignity.

His recycling basket abruptly came to mind, and she smiled. She'd been touched to know he was trying to be environmentally responsible. Could he actually be trying to please her too?

If only he could . . . care. Really care. She wanted him so desperately, she'd risk it all if he loved her just a little.

"Snap out of it, dammit," she muttered out loud. Loving Miles was a bad investment. He was too cold and ruthless to know how to love back.

She should face the fact that she was just as bad as he was in a lot of ways. Witness what she was doing now. Somehow the Earth Angel stunts had a lot more integrity attached to them than a knock-down-drag-out board fight. Something else bothered her about Miles's plan. Something that had nothing to do with her family or working with him. She wished she knew what it was.

But what other option was there? She couldn't think of even one.

The telephone rang. She didn't feel like answering it, but decided she probably should. When she picked up the receiver, she discovered Miles on the other end of the line. She really ought to cut down on following her impulses, she thought.

"Have you changed your mind?" he asked, his voice sounding like fine wine. It hurt to hear it, even as she drank it in.

"No."

"Are you going to walk out of my office again if I say something disagreeable?"

"No."

"Hang up the telephone?"

"No."

"Are you—"

"Miles, I'm not in the mood for Twenty Questions." She rubbed the ache from her forehead. "What do you want?"

"We didn't finish our discussion."

"I thought we had."

"I think we should be talking about a CEO for you, who will do the day-to-day running of the company. I have someone in mind."

"Aren't you rushing things?"

"I'm thinking ahead." He paused. "I also called my banking consortium. They will leave Wagner Oil to my discretion for the moment."

The plan was already moving forward, and she wasn't ready for it. She sighed. "Okay."

"This media reception is the time for you to really make an impression. It's also the time for me to begin my end of the campaign. Do you know who's going to be there?"

"Yes. The three networks and CNN are sending people, plus all the major newspapers. And city, state, and federal politicians are coming, even some environmental people. Uncle Byrne is flipping between conniption fits and overseeing every little detail of the reception."

"Perfect. You can make a great debut. Be sure to talk to all of them. Say the right things."

"Would you like to write them out for me?" she asked dryly.

"No. I trust you."

She looked heavenward and shook her head. He'd turn into Vince Lombardy before the reception rolled around.

"Catherine, I'm sorry I caused you . . . pain before. I never meant to."

His apology so surprised her, she couldn't speak for a minute.

"Catherine?"

"Yes." She cleared her throat. This was so unlike him, she didn't know what to say. "I . . . Thank you, Miles."

"Why don't you retake the bar? There's no limit to the number of times you can take it, right?"

"There is a limit to the number of times a person will humiliate herself," she pointed out.

"You'll pass. There's no reason why you can't. Or is it that you don't really want to?"

"I've asked myself the same question over the years," she admitted, smiling wryly. "I don't have any desire to be a lawyer any longer. At least I don't think I do."

"You'd scare the pants off me if you were my opponent's counsel." He paused, and when he spoke again, his voice was deep and serious. "Here comes the 'don't hang up' part. Catherine, I miss you and I want you to come back."

She gripped the receiver tightly against the temptation. "No."

"You're punishing me for something that happened years ago. I'm not the same person I was then. Hell, Catherine, I might have been detached about a lot of things at that time, but I don't think I was the person you thought I was. I know I never would have been with you. You are not a one-night-stand woman."

His words cut through the steel around her heart. She willed herself to stay calm. He was the wrong man for her, and she would not follow something that was doomed before it even started. "I'm not punishing you, Miles. But that incident did show me that your moral values and mine are vastly different."

"I can't make up for it, and I am *not* going to apologize for being so attracted to you that I acted on impulse. I certainly didn't do it to insult you. All I'm asking for is time to let this new relationship grow between us. Why is that so bad? Why do you want to rush something just for the sake of commitment?"

"I'm not rushing anything," she denied, even as she wondered if he was right. "I'm afraid you're incapable of making a commitment."

"That was blunt enough." He was silent for a moment. "What will break the impasse between us?"

"I don't know," she said honestly. She was tired of fighting him. She had to, though, for her own sanity. "I don't know that there's anything that can. It's not an impasse. It's a fact of life. Goodbye, Miles."

She set the receiver back in its cradle.

"Catherine! What the hell are you wearing?"

Miles stared open-mouthed at Catherine's gown.

The brocade material had jeweled threads running through it, giving the long slim skirt a glittering look. But the gown completely backless, and the V neckline in the front plunged so deep, it exposed the inner curves of her breasts. She looked absolutely stunning, elegant, sophisticated, and sexy. Too sexy. They were standing in the foyer of the hotel ballroom where the media reception was being held, and she was already attracting attention. Twin urges run rampant through him. One was to kill any man who feasted his gaze on what belonged to him, and the other was to make love to her.

After that first painful conversation a few days ago, they had had several more congenial ones. He'd hung in there, courting her slowly. But not once had she mentioned this dress!

She smiled innocently as she tucked her oversized evening bag under her arm. "It's a gown, Miles. You know what they are. Ankle-length dress, lots of material, very dramatic."

"It looks like a shortfall of material to me," he said. He should have known disaster was looming when she'd been late arriving. He pulled her off to the side of the foyer, far away from lecherous eyes. "I should have approved your clothes for tonight."

She eyed him. "Don't even think it, Miles."

He took a deep breath. He had a big job to do here, both of them did. They ought to be talking about that, not about a dress that made him sigh in pleasure and growl in possession. But he couldn't let it go. "You're not going in like that."

She blinked. "Miles, *you* wanted me to look my best. This is my best."

"Damn straight it is," he muttered. "I don't like it."

"You don't get a vote." She whirled on her peacock-blue heels and walked into the reception.

He followed behind her, frowning darkly. He should have picked her up at her house, and he should have made damn sure she never left it. Jealously, pure and simple, was what he was suffering from. The experience was new.

Everything about Catherine was new—including the shock from their past. She *was* punishing him. That small piece of youthful impulse had cost him dearly. Now he would have to earn her back. Unfortunately, he had no idea how.

Inside the ballroom, a string orchestra played energetic music, and voices and laughter swelled above the violins. He caught up with Catherine.

"Now, Catherine—" he began.

She interrupted. "Miles, I don't want to hear it, okay?"

"And I don't want men seeing you, wanting you . . ." Why couldn't she see the point he was making? "That dress is . . . Oh, hell, you look fabulous and I hate it."

Her mouth gaped open in astonishment. He felt stupid, like a young teenager with his first girl.

"Hi, are we having fun yet?" Catherine's aunt Sylvia asked, coming up at precisely the wrong moment.

Miles forced himself to smile at her. "We're jumping with joy. Everybody looks jovial, though."

"So far," Sylvia said, pleased. "The media is eating and drinking up everything in sight. I hope full stomachs put them in a contented mood."

"It looks more like they're vultures circling the carcass," Catherine said wryly.

"Byrne will make it that way," Miles said absent-mindedly, noticing two men staring at Catherine. He glared at them until they looked away.

"Byrne is a walking disaster," Sylvia said, looking worried.

It's showtime, Miles thought.

"Well," he began expansively, doing another Ronald Reagan imitation. "I hope all this comes off the way it should. The bank consortium is not pleased with the way Byrne has handled the corporation's public image. They want changes."

Sylvia's frown of worry deepened. "We've got some big loans with them right now, too."

Miles smiled. Out of the corner of his eye, he saw Catherine's lips thin into a grim line. She might not like it, but it had to be done. "Yes," he answered Sylvia. "If this keeps up, they are not going to be happy . . . or cooperative."

"Excuse me," Catherine said. "I see some people I should talk to."

Miles smothered a grimace when she walked away. He had a feeling she would be doing that the entire evening. It was more of an advantage, though, to talk to Sylvia alone.

"And if it does keep up, Miles?" Sylvia asked.

She reminded him of Catherine in some ways, he mused. She was as straightforward. "They're going to ask for some management changes. Some board changes, to be honest. And if you can't make the balloon payment coming up, they won't have to ask. They'll be the ones doing it."

The older woman swallowed. "Will they negotiate an extension?"

"I won't recommend that to them," he said flatly. "Not with the nonsense Byrne is pulling. Byrne is not his father. The change Wagner Oil needs is at the top."

Sylvia took a deep breath. "I know."

Miles looked toward Catherine. "Catherine is young . . . but she makes a lot of sense."

"I know." Sylvia smiled.

Miles smiled back. His message was received.

"Wagner Oil is not responding completely to these accusations from the Earth Angel. By the way, that's a gorgeous gown."

Catherine smiled at Mariana Tolliver. Channel Five's beautiful investigative reporter was on the attack tonight. "We are repairing the leaks and cleaning up those drums, Mariana. And we're correcting all our procedures to ensure such problems never happen again. The dress is a Sidney Marshall."

Catherine hid a smile, remembering Mile's reaction to the dress. She half felt she'd picked it just to provoke his response. And she was half pleased that he had acted a bit possessive.

"I knew it," Mariana said, grinning. "She's a wonderful designer. I kill for her stuff. How do you explain how those 'problems' happened in the first place?"

"You've got a Mike Wallace—Coco Chanel technique," Catherine said, chuckling. "You've had the company's official statement concerning the problems. As an officer of the corporation, I stand by it."

"And I so liked your dress." The woman sighed. "Come on, Catherine, don't you evade too."

"How about if I take you on a plant tour?" Catherine suggested. The more open she was, the more the reporter would assume there was no nasty hidden story to be had. And at least it took her mind off Miles, Catherine thought. She had been evading him for the past hour, only to realize he was with one of her relatives after another, "doing business." It still hurt.

"Can I poke anywhere I want?" Mariana asked.

"As long as it's not an EPA restricted zone," Catherine answered. "We've been fined enough."

Mariana laughed. "I suppose I can agree to that."

"I'm eternally grateful."

Mariana took a bite of her crab pastry. "You people are going all out in this congenial bribe."

"And you people are certainly eating it up," Catherine replied with an easy laugh.

She suddenly felt a presence close behind her. She didn't have to see the sudden interest in Mariana's gaze to know who it was. An instant internal matching was going on inside her body, and there was only one man she matched so instantly with. Miles.

"Mr. Kitteridge," Mariana said, her smile sickeningly sweet. "Wagner Oil has outdone itself tonight. I've been talking with Catherine here about what the company is doing to improve its image."

"Catherine is certainly the one to answer that," Miles said smoothly. "She is an expert on environmental safety procedures, and she's been instrumental in the changes you've been witnessing tonight."

Catherine nearly choked. He hit a little too close to home with that one.

Mariana asked the same questions of Miles that she had of Catherine. She glanced at him as he answered, and the questions that had been bothering her lately resurfaced. Was she punishing him for before? She didn't think so. Had he changed? He fed her cold remedies galore, apologized, even got arrested for her. He asked her to come back. At the same time, he was the moving force behind a brewing board fight to put her into the chairmanship of Wagner Oil. And not once had he said he loved her.

". . . and she's taking me on a tour of the refinery. No doors barred."

The words brought Catherine's attention back to the conversation, and she held her breath, waiting for Miles's answer. He wouldn't like this, she was sure.

"Great," he said, without even a blink. "As a matter of fact, Wagner will be getting into the environmental cleanup business. The company intends to lead the way in this field. Could I steal Catherine away from you?"

"But . . . but . . ." Mariana sputtered.

Catherine found herself dragged away by Miles's firm grip on her arm before the woman could protest. She couldn't get a protest in anywhere, either—not without giving Mariana something to investigate. The wild delight she felt at his hand on her bare flesh only added to her confusion.

"Since when did we get into the cleanup business?" she asked.

"Since I found out how lucrative it's becoming,"

he replied. "It'll be one of the first things you institute when you're chairperson."

She narrowed her eyes. It wasn't his company, but clearly he thought it was going to be. "What else will *I* be instituting?"

He grinned. "Whatever will make money. Responsibly, of course."

She didn't like the sound of this. "Where are we going?"

"I want to talk to you alone." He grimaced. "And I'm damn sick and tired of the men here ogling you. Can you stuff a napkin in there or something?"

She looked heavenward. "No."

"I was afraid you'd say that." He maneuvered them into a quiet corner. As he gazed down at her, her breath caught. Suddenly she wished she did have that napkin. She braced herself for him to touch her, but all he said was, "I've talked to the other board members, and they're all disturbed by Byrne."

"And you gave them the consortium pressure, I'm sure," she said, her conflicting emotions hardening her voice.

"You're being prickly again." He smiled. "We've got to use all the tools we can. I want you to talk to them about some of those safety procedures you mentioned before—"

She interrupted. "I'm going to talk to them about saving the Utah land."

"The Utah land? Oh. From the codicil. I forgot. They may just be ripe for that, especially if you point out how it will be a show of our good environmental faith."

He was amazing, she thought. And *very* full of

plans on her behalf. What had been bothering her in this board fight beyond the family ties became crystal clear. She was going to be a puppet chairperson, with Miles running the works behind the scenes.

"Catherine," he said seriously, abruptly changing the subject, "being apart isn't solving anything. Come home with me tonight. We need to talk . . . about us."

His words rang harshly in her head. Of course, she realized suddenly. He had never asked her to stay or to come back until after he had thought up this plan for a Wagner board shake-up. *After.* She was being used.

The room squeezed in on her, tilting and fading to near black.

"Catherine?" His voice came from far away.

He touched her arm. It was like a slap of icy water. She wouldn't let the pain show, she thought. Two could play his game.

"Not tonight," she said, her voice sounding remarkably normal. "It wouldn't be good for us to be seen together too much. Everyone thinks we're lovers now, but it's better to confuse them. Keep them off balance. You work the crowd your way, and I'll work them mine, okay?"

"But—"

She patted his cheek. "We'll talk later. I have to arrange Mariana's tour."

With that, she walked away.

It was Earth Angel's swan song.

Very carefully, Catherine set the jar of sludge on the buffet table. For the past half hour the table had been swamped by a steady stream of media people, until she'd thought she would go crazy with the waiting. She had nearly left, so distraught by Miles's manipulations. Nearly. Finally the feeding frenzy had slowed, and she had casually wandered over.

The jar wasn't big, just a quart-size mayonnaise one that had fit in her velvet bag. The sludge was straight from Wagner's refinery drain, and the jar was clearly marked and signed by the lab that had tested it.

She had debated over whether or not to do this. It would be extremely risky, but the opportunity was too good to resist. A final mission, a most dramatic one—and one that would tweak a certain nose or two. She hadn't been able to resist that, either.

She stood in front of the jar and glanced around to see if anyone was watching her. No one paid any attention.

Perfect.

She strolled away.

Miles heard the commotion by the buffet table before he saw it. People were looking and pointing and buzzing—and laughing in satisfied amusement.

"What's going on?" the state senator Miles was talking to asked.

Miles shrugged, slightly annoyed to have his chat with the man interrupted. "I don't know."

The laughter rose. He and the senator wandered over. He couldn't get close enough to see anything at first, then the crowd shifted enough for him to spy an innocent looking jar of brown mud.

"The Earth Angel!" somebody said.

"Let me through!" Byrne shouted. "Turn off those cameras! Let me through!"

Instead, the reporters crowded around him. all of them babbling questions. "Help!" Byrne squawked. "Get away, get away!"

Miles turned on his heel and strode across the vast ballroom. His aim was unerring. That damn dress was hard to miss.

So was Catherine's completely innocent expression when he reached her.

"Welcome home, sweetheart," he said, before she could say a word.

He took her by the arm and hauled her out of the reception.

Ten

"I'm not going to your house again."

Catherine instantly wanted to take back the words at the look Miles gave her.

"You will," he said tersely, pushing her past several guests leaving the reception and into the elevator. It was an express. He jabbed the button that closed the doors, saying to the others, "Sorry. It's full."

The people stared open-mouthed. The doors slid shut.

Catherine had never seen him so angry before. Maybe, she mused, she might have gone a little too far this time.

"Miles—"

"Catherine, don't," he said, his voice so cold it could have refrozen the arctic.

She swallowed hard. If she would ever know when to keep quiet rather than fight, this was definitely the moment.

The elevator ride was made in deadly silence. So was the wait for his Corvette to be brought around. Catherine shivered in the cool September air. She thought of her evening coat back in the cloakroom and decided it wasn't worth mentioning.

Without a word, Miles shed his tuxedo jacket and dropped it around her shoulders like a sack of potatoes.

"We will go to my house and we will have this out," he announced abruptly. "You broke the deal, Catherine. Again."

All the defiance went out of her when she realized Miles was a thread away from losing his control. Smothering the urge to tell him why she had done what she'd done, she pulled the jacket tight around her shoulders. She felt cocooned in his body heat. The so-familiar scent of him enveloped her, and pain knifed through her at the thought of what she wanted and couldn't have.

In the car, conversation was nearly nonexistent and tension was tantamount.

At one point, she did ask, "Do you think our disappearance might cause some talk?"

"I doubt it. You saw fit to take care of that," he said coldly.

The car screeched to a halt at his front door. She had just touched the door handle when her car door was wrenched open. Miles had come around the car that fast.

She scooted past him when he opened the house door, then jumped and spun around when he slammed it shut behind them.

He looked about to explode.

"Now, Miles . . ." she began, backing away from him.

He stalked her. "Why? Just tell me why you pulled this stunt that could ruin everything."

"Nobody saw me."

"There were over two hundred people in that room!" he roared. "How could you *not* be seen?"

"I checked," she said, glancing around for an escape route. None was available.

"You better hope to heaven you weren't seen. Because if you were—"

"If I was, the phone would be ringing off the hook already for a statement from you." She rushed on with her explanation. "Miles, it was my last time as the Earth Angel. Truly. I wasn't going to do it at all. Honest. But this has been too important not to use such an event to make a point—"

"A point!" He gaped at her. "I have been working my tail off to get you a legitimate forum for your cause, and you sabotage me."

"I wasn't trying to sabotage you. I didn't want the family to become complacent . . ." The look on his face shook her. She scrambled for a better explanation as anxiety mingled with anticipation. "I mean, I . . . It was . . ."

"You did it just to be obtuse."

She wondered if she had. She had known he would figure out who did it. And she had known somewhere inside her exactly what he would do—bring her to his home and keep her under twenty-four-hour surveillance. The two of them alone.

He backed her against the wall, pressing so close, a sheet of paper couldn't have been wedged between them. "Dammit, Catherine. If I say the car is black, you automatically say it's white. If I ask you to do something or not do something, it's because I care about your welfare. But you have defied me at every turn and treated me like I'm the muck from the bottom of a pond. I'll tell you who the pond scum was: that philanthropic jerk you keep on a pedestal. He was using you for a meal ticket and you still can't see it. You make me insane with jealousy and drive me crazy in general, and I don't know why the hell I put up with it except that I love you—"

Catherine gasped at the shocking words. There was no doubting they were unprepared, unrehearsed, and totally genuine. *Genuine.* Her wall of resistance crumbled away.

Miles stopped his tirade and stared dumbfounded at her. All of his anger dissolved as the truth of what he'd said rocked him to his roots.

"Do you mean it?" she asked.

"I guess so." He smiled, then laughed. Suddenly, everything made so much sense. He must have been blind not to see it before. "Oh, hell, Catherine, it figures."

He touched her cheek, the softness of her skin springing up a well of desire in him.

"You don't sound very happy about it," she whispered.

He grinned wryly. "I'm not sure I should be. Will you marry me?"

Her jaw dropped in complete astonishment. His grin widened.

"You can't mean it," she said, shaking her head.

His heart skipped a beat. "I'd be a fool to let you get away a second time. I nearly was. Besides, you need a keeper, and I don't know how else to do it." He grew serious. "You'll learn to love me, Catherine. I promise."

She was silent for a long moment, then looked straight at him. "I already do."

His whole world tilted at the wonderful words, then snapped back into place. He kissed her, and her mouth instantly surrendered to his. All of her seemed to surrender in his embrace. She had never felt so soft and gentle with him before.

Everything went out of his head except her revelation. He didn't care how she had come to love him, it only mattered that she did. He wanted her so badly. All the lost days and nights needed to be erased in an intimate confirmation of their words.

He broke the kiss and lifted her in his arms. She was solid and real, and he turned and carried her up the stairs.

"What are you doing?" she asked, clinging deliciously to his shoulders.

"Rhett Butler imitations," he answered, holding her tightly against him.

"Just don't get a hernia."

"It's not in the script."

She smiled. "You really know how to end a fight."

He smiled in return. "This is just the break between rounds. I'm still furious with you, but we'll argue later. First, we'll learn to trust each other."

"Can we?"

The question was hesitant, and he heard the desperation in her voice.

"We can," he assured her. "We have a lifetime to do it in."

It occurred to him that she hadn't answered his proposal, but by then he'd reached his bedroom. Catherine was in his arms, in love with him, and he knew he already had his answer.

He kept one arm around her bare back, but let go of her legs, her thighs sliding against his and taking his breath away at the same moment.

He ran his hands along her spine, her flesh like silk under his fingers. "I think I asked you into my bed those years ago to keep you from marrying the pond scum."

"It took you long enough to do anything about it," she said, unfastening his shirt studs.

"You didn't help matters." He unhooked the halter from around her neck. The bodice dropped to her waist, exposing her breasts to his gaze. Her nipples were tight already.

"Never," he said hoarsely, "wear this dress again for anyone except me."

"Never," she promised, pushing his shirt open. She rubbed her breasts against his chest. "I love you, Miles."

His control broke. He took her lips in an all-encompassing kiss. Her tongue mated with his, driving him to the brink of insanity. She would always do that to him, and he didn't want it any other way. He loved her.

Clothes disappeared in a frenzy of hands. Every touch was a renewal and discovery. Every kiss a commitment. Catherine became one with him, each thrust a wild promise of the future.

And all wrapped in the passion was the tender thread of love.

Catherine slowly surfaced. Morning sunlight streamed through the windows. Her first thought was that it had all been a dream. Her second was the realization that she was in Miles's bed, naked and contented, lying atop a naked and contented Miles.

Everything came rushing back to her.

He had said words she never thought she'd hear from him. It was what she had wanted for so long, and her willpower had dissolved instantly. She had no doubt that he did love her. She smiled to herself, remembering that he'd been as surprised as she at the spontaneous acknowledgment.

"What's so funny?" he asked, his voice husky with sleep.

"Just thinking," she murmured, recalling, too, the way he had whispered "I love you" later like a litany. No, like a discovery of something wonderful. The words had touched her so deeply, she had been branded by them. How could she not be?

"Thinking is dangerous," he said. "Especially with you."

"Are you starting another fight?"

He grinned and ran his hand along her backside. "Only if we can make up like this." His grin faded. "Catherine, promise me Earth Angel has made her last protest. Ever."

"I promise."

"I'm trusting you to keep it this time."

"I'll keep it."

Her throat tightened, though. There was that word. "Trust." She believed he loved her, but she was almost afraid to take that first tentative step toward trust. He had said he was a changed man from before. He had been very solicitous when he'd thought she was ill. He had spoken out at the board meetings for environmental changes. He had even put up the sign and got arrested for her. She had to admit he was meeting her halfway. She could only do the same. Besides, if they were ever going to trust each other, it had to start now.

"Catherine, you never answered my proposal."

The hesitancy in his voice was obvious. She glanced at him and saw his worried expression. It figured, she thought. Now she found herself reluctant to make a commitment.

"I thought you wanted to see where the relationship was going," she said.

He smiled sheepishly. "I didn't want to rush you. I know what I want, and I don't want to lose you. I love you. Marry me."

If she said yes, her surrender to him would be complete.

She drew in a deep breath. "Yes."

He pulled her into his arms and kissed her. Her head was spinning by the time he released her.

"Just don't ever say no," he whispered, nuzzling her throat.

Sensual pleasure surged through her, and she couldn't think straight. She didn't want to.

Much later, Miles said, "I wonder how the reception went after we left."

"We could always have hung around," she commented.

"You probably would have stood on a table and announced you were the Earth Angel."

"Mmmm. Now there's a thought."

"Catherine," he began in warning.

She laughed and snuggled in his arms.

"As long as it's only a thought." He was silent for a moment. "When we left, Byrne was making a complete fool of himself with the media."

She shuddered, thinking of the news reports.

"We had better get started taking advantage of

that," Miles went on. "Once we get you installed as chairperson, I'll call Bob Ross from Kimble Industries. He owes me for a bank deal, so I think I can lure him away to become Wagner's chief executive officer . . ."

Catherine shut her eyes. Miles hadn't changed all that much. Clearly, he was on a course that would give him behind-the-scenes control of Wagner Oil. She couldn't allow that. She had to believe he loved her. There was just too much evidence proving it. She wanted desperately to trust him, to trust that his marriage proposal wasn't connected in any way to the business. She wanted to know she had surrendered everything to a man who wanted her for herself.

What she needed was proof.

". . . I've looked at the corporation bylaws," he was saying, "and two directors can also call an emergency meeting. I think you and I can do that. Everyone was more than ready to remove Byrne when I talked to them last night. I think they've all seen the light."

A brilliant idea flashed through her head. Catherine swallowed back a jolt of fear, but it grew in her mind, clicking into place like the last pieces of a puzzle. It would put the company into caring hands, and prove whether or not his proposal was motivated by business. If he truly loved her, he would even understand. And if he didn't . . .

She only hoped Miles would see the light after she was done.

The atmosphere in the conference room was grim.

Miles glanced around at the faces of the Wagner board of directors. Each one was set with a cold expression—except Byrne's. He was sweating profusely. Miles almost felt sorry for the man. The various newspapers on the conference table were filled with his attack on the media at the reception. The videotapes next to the newspapers were worse, with the TV news reports of Byrne's performance. He and Catherine had missed quite a show, evidently.

She sat across from him now, looking quiet, subdued, and beautiful in a pale green outfit. Only Catherine could turn soft colors into a power suit, he mused. He knew she was nervous and unsure of her abilities to chair Wagner Oil. But he knew different, and he had never been prouder of her. She had fought him every step of the way, but now it was over and she was his. He still felt as if he'd been hit on the forehead with a sledgehammer and the granite had fallen away from his eyes. She was a unique woman, and the moment he'd said he loved her, he'd known that was what had been happening all along.

People at the table looked expectantly at him. He and Catherine had spent two days huddled in separate rooms, talking the relatives into this meeting. They all wanted it short and sweet. As the director who'd called the meeting, Miles cleared his throat and opened it. "It is obvious that board management at Wagner Oil cannot continue as it has. We have to change our tactics, our entire method of doing business, and we need someone who understands that."

"That's been very obvious for a long time," Catherine's father said.

Miles smothered a wry smile. When the man came around, he really came around. He still wasn't quite convinced that his own daughter was the best choice, but he was convinced the bank held the voting strings.

"We'll lose our shirts," Byrne said, smacking the table with his palm.

"We're already losing them," Catherine said coolly.

"And Wagner cannot afford to lose more," Miles said, turning to Byrne. "I'm sorry, Byrne, but I have no choice but to call for your resignation."

"No! No!" Byrne shouted, banging on the table.

"A resignation would be best for you," Sylvia said, sympathy in her voice. "You know we're in trouble, and we all know you want what's best for Wagner Oil."

"You're all just jealous of me because Father put me in charge." Byrne's eyes were bulging. "You always have been."

Miles shook his head. "Allan wasn't my father, Byrne. I have no ties. I move Byrne be removed from the board of directors.

Several voices sounded. Privately, Miles was relieved there was more than one. There would be fewer hard feelings afterward. "All in favor?" he asked.

The ayes were firm and nearly unanimous. Byrne collapsed in defeat. Nobody looked at him. Nobody said a word. He got up and left the room, finally gaining the dignity he had needed as chairman. Even though he knew it was the only option, Miles couldn't help feeling guilty.

From across the table, Catherine looked sadly at him, and he smiled to reassure her. To his surprise, there were tears in her eyes. He had known this action upset her, but he hadn't expected her to react like this. If she blamed him . . . he didn't think he could handle it.

"Uncle Byrne will still receive his salary and bonuses in a stock and profit-sharing package," she said.

Miles nodded. "Agreed."

He would find out in another second if his life was in ruin, he thought, realizing it was time to nominate her. He opened his mouth.

"I nominate Sylvia for the post of chairperson."

Miles blinked. The voice wasn't his, and the name wasn't the one he'd expected to say. It was Catherine who spoke.

Everything inside him went cold.

"Second!"

The voices were fast and furious. Miles stared around the table, bewildered by the turn of events and unable to stop them. No one would look directly at him. Instead, they deliberately looked away.

"All in favor?" Catherine asked.

"Aye." Every damn one of them said it.

"Catherine!" Miles roared, realizing she had engineered a coup behind his back.

She never flinched, as the rest of her family practically ducked for cover. "I had to, Miles. You were planning to control the company through me. I couldn't allow that."

"I was not!" He leaped to his feet, shoving back his chair. "Never would I do something so underhanded, but you can't help thinking that, can you?"

"Miles, unconsciously you were," she replied, her

voice steady. "Think of all the plans you had for me—"

"To help you!"

She smiled sadly. "You would have been running the show, even if you didn't realize it."

"Why didn't you tell me of your concerns about my running the corporation through you?"

She didn't answer.

"The consortium won't tolerate it," he reminded her.

"Yes, they will," she shot back confidently. "Sylvia is much more competent and experienced than I am, and she understands the need for environmental safety and for developing new fuels. She's the *best* person for the chairmanship. And you'll grant the extension because the consortium can't really afford the loss if we folded, and you know it. Miles, I love you. I needed to know you love me for me, not anything to do with Wagner Oil."

The words were a slap in the face.

"This is a damned test, isn't it?" he asked, furious.

"I—I have to know," she said, lifting her chin.

She was so beautiful and so treacherous, he thought. And she had played him for a fool. Well, she'd done it for the last time.

"You hand me all this bull," he said, "about trust and commitment, but you're the one who can't trust and you're the one who can't make a commitment. You're the one who can't pass the test, Catherine."

He stalked out of the room.

Now she knew.

Catherine swiped at the renewed tears, angry

that she didn't seem to be able to stop them. This time it was Miles who wasn't answering calls. He wasn't at the house, either. Or so his housekeeper said when she'd gone there. Miles seemed to have vanished off the face of Philadelphia.

Maybe it was for the better, she thought, rolling over on her bed. What could she have said to him, anyway? He must hate her for what she'd done. And yet she hadn't known what else to do. She didn't have enough experience or knowledge to have kept him from running Wagner Oil, if that was what he'd wanted. And she had to be sure there was no business in the marriage proposal. Why couldn't he understand that?

The telephone rang, and she snatched it up, her heart pounding excitedly. "Hello."

"My grandson has disappeared for the last two days," Lettice said. "The bank's been calling, looking for him."

Catherine's heart sank. "I don't know where he is. We—we had a fight."

"A board fight." Lettice harrumphed in disapproval. "I heard about it from your aunt Sylvia. I leave you two alone, and you make a hash of everything."

"I didn't make a hash," Catherine began, then sighed. "I did. Lettice, I . . . Miles was going to run the company through me. At least, that's how he made everything sound. I couldn't let him do that."

"Of course you couldn't, dear," Lettice said. "It would be just like him, and he'd never realize it. He always was a controller. That's why he's such a good banker. Your job was to snap him out of it.

That's why you're so good for him. And he's good for you."

Catherine paused. "But we're so different."

"Naturally. It makes life exciting." Lettice was quiet for a long moment. "Never *ever* let that get away from you."

Catherine understood the words completely. "I should have told Miles how I felt. I wasn't ready for the job."

"Well, he's a steamroller at times. So go and find him and explain."

Catherine broke into fresh tears. "But I did explain. At the meeting. And he stormed off."

"Typical. So go find him and seduce him. He's bound to forgive you after that."

"But that's the point, dammit! I don't know where to look."

"Try his club, or the house we have in Maine. He's been known to go there upon occasion. He may have even gone to his brother Devlin's. In fact, try there first. If he's there, he ought to be more than ready to come home . . ."

A strange noise began to filter through her windows. Someone was playing a boom box with the volume turned up to maximum. Still listening but barely able to hear Lettice rattling off more places where she could find Miles, Catherine got up to close the windows until the rude and very deaf person passed by.

Then she realized the rude and deaf person was playing "Earth Angel."

She pushed aside the curtains and looked out. There on the pavement below her was Miles, sitting on the open top of a limousine with a boom box blaring and a huge bouquet of flowers on his lap. A group had gathered around the limo, and in true Philadelphia fashion, people were dancing.

She dropped the phone, flung up her window screen, and stuck her head out. "Miles! Miles!"

He turned down the volume. Peace filled the air, broken only by the groans of the dancers.

"What are you doing?" she called out.

He grinned at her. "Coming after you. I figured if it was good enough for Richard Gere, then it's good enough for me. Besides, if I waited for you, I'd be a dead man."

"I couldn't find you." The tears started again. She pushed them away with her fingers.

"I was . . . thinking at my brother's, but I hate—" His words were overrun by the dancers calling for him to turn the music back on.

Catherine frowned. She thought he'd said "fish," but couldn't be sure. It didn't matter.

"I love you. Can I come in?" he shouted.

"Oh!" She laughed. "Yes!"

Everyone applauded.

She raced down the stairs and opened the front door. Miles was already there. The music was playing again behind him. He stepped inside, pulled her into his arms, and slammed the door shut.

"Miles, I'm sorry," she whispered, just before his mouth covered hers.

The kiss was filled with longing and love. It rocked through her like a tidal wave, and she clung to him, feeling the strong flesh and bone so real beneath her fingers.

Finally he lifted his head. "Maybe you were a little right about my trying to run the company."

"I suppose that's about as far as you'll go with an apology," she murmured, kissing his cheek.

"Just about," he agreed, his voice hoarse with growing passion. "I didn't realize what I was doing, Catherine. You were right about Sylvia. She'll be excellent."

"I know." She ran her hands down his shirt-front. "Next time, I'll talk to you first. I should have told you how I felt. I was unfair to you. I do trust you, Miles."

He chuckled dryly. "There's nothing left to *not* trust me with."

"My heart is left," she corrected him. "It's the most vulnerable of all."

He held her tightly. "I'll keep it safe next to mine."

"That's all I ask."

When they surfaced again, he said, "Let's go. The limo's waiting."

"Where are we going?"

"To my house, where you belong."

She smiled. Then she remembered. "Your grand-mother. She's on the phone."

"She'll hang up eventually."

"But the bank's looking for you."

He opened the front door. "It can wait. I can't. We have to go do something very natural and environ-mentally safe."

"My, you have changed."

"All from the love of a good woman. And you are very good. Promise you'll drive me crazy for the rest of my life."

She grinned. "I guarantee it."

Epilogue

"Wagner Oil is up four points on the market."

Catherine swung around from the bath she was filling. Miles stood in the doorway, holding a newspaper.

"Give me that thing," she said, snatching it out of his hands. She flipped it open. "We agreed no business at the cabin on the honeymoon. Anyway, how did you arrange to have it delivered . . . . Wait a minute. This is last week's newspaper."

He shrugged. "I needed a fix. Take me outside and let me bask in the real fresh air and sunshine and it'll go away."

"You're naked," she pointed out.

He looked down at himself, then shrugged again and rubbed his chest. "Clothes take a lot of energy to be manufactured, and then there's the dyes polluting the atmosphere—"

"They pollute the water."

"The water. Not to mention the impact to the landfills when they're thrown away . . ."

She reached down and turned off the taps. "I'll

buy you a lifetime membership in a nature club. Happy now?"

"Ecstatic."

She dropped her robe and stepped into the old-fashioned claw-footed tub. Sighing, she lay back in the warm water, the liquid like silk against her skin.

Miles walked over to the tub and climbed in with her. "Shall we conserve?"

"You're a fast learner," she murmured.

The past week had been sheer bliss, and Catherine had no doubt Miles was enjoying every minute of it, business fix or not. She vowed to make up for every hurt she'd caused him. And *she* would love every minute of that.

That afternoon, as they sat on the cabin porch, Miles plucked at his flannel shirt and grumbled, "Too damned confining."

She grinned at him. "What are you going to do when you get back into your three-piece suits?"

"Itch to death." He glanced out at the spectacular view of Utah's Wah Wah mountain range. The peaks were capped white and plunged into deep sand valleys. The blue-green haze of Sevier Lake was just visible in the distance. Clouds danced across a pristine sky. "I bet there isn't another human within twenty miles of this little cabin. I still can't believe anyone was ready to turn this place into a strip mine. It would have been a sin."

"Not anyone, Miles. Us," she said gently, leaning on the porch rail. "And you stopped it. Without the codicil."

He nodded, feeling a little like Superman. "Glad I was finally able to see the place."

She turned and looked at him. "That's right. You

hadn't seen it. I knew what I was fighting for because I'd come up here with Grandfather. But you didn't. You even put up that sign and didn't know what it said."

He chuckled. "I had great faith in you."

To his surprise, she flung herself against him. "I . . . Miles, you did. I never realized. I promise I'll make it up to you."

"You already did," he said, wrapping his arms around her. "You married me against your better judgment."

"I have lousy judgment."

"Excuse me, folks."

Miles turned to find Mr. Walters, a fishing friend of Allan's who took care of the cabin, puffing his way toward them. Catherine slipped out of his arms. So much for his theory about twenty miles.

"Left my truck at the bottom of the canyon and climbed up," Walters said, taking off his cowboy hat and wiping his forehead. "Didn't think Red would make it. I damn near didn't, either." He held out a large envelope. "This come for you two. It looks important, so I thought I better bring it right away."

Catherine took the envelope from him. Miles looked at the return address and raised his eyebrows. "It's from Grandmother."

Catherine pulled open the gummed flap and shook out a legal looking document.

"Must be another one of her friend's schemes she wants me to approve," he said, looking over his wife's shoulder.

"Miles." Catherine's voice shook. "It's the missing codicil."

Miles read the first paragraph more closely. It

was. He pulled off the frilly notepaper clipped to it and read aloud:

Dear Catherine and Miles,

It was quite a fight to get you two together, but you both *finally* came around. Here is the codicil from Allan. He left it in my keeping to file, not trusting his lawyers. I'm afraid I fibbed a little about a few things. I *had* to do something to get you involved with each other. You were too slow on your own. Allan would be pleased to know he had a hand in some matchmaking. Know you'll forgive my small deception because it all turned out right in the end. Love, Grandmother.

Miles crumpled the note and tossed it over the edge of the canyon. "I think I'll kill her when we get home."

"I get to go first." Catherine carefully folded the document. "We better get home and file this with the state."

"After we do something natural and environmentally safe," Miles reminded her.

Mr. Walters frowned in puzzlement.

Three thousand miles away, Lettice smiled.

THE EDITOR'S CORNER

And what is so rare as a day in June?
Then, if ever, come perfect days . . .

With apologies to James Russell Lowell I believe we can add *and perfect reading, too,* from LOVESWEPT and FANFARE . . .

As fresh and beautiful as the rose in its title SAN ANTONIO ROSE, LOVESWEPT #474, by Fran Baker is a thrilling way to start your romance reading next month. Rafe Martinez betrayed Jeannie Crane, but her desire still burned for the only man she'd ever loved, the only man who'd ever made love to her. Rafe was back and admitting to her that her own father had driven him away. When he learned her secret, Rafe had a sure-fire way to get revenge . . . but would he? And could Jeannie ever find a way to tame the maverick who still drove her wild with ecstasy? This unforgettable love story will leave you breathless. . . .

Perfect in its powerful emotion is TOUGH GUY, SAVVY LADY, LOVESWEPT #475, by Charlotte Hughes. Charlotte tells a marvelous story of overwhelming love and stunning self-discovery in this tale of beautiful Honey Buchannan and Lucas McKay. Lucas smothered her with his love, sweetly dominating her life—and when she leaves he is distraught, but determined to win her back. Lucas has always hidden his own fears—he's a man who has pulled himself up by his boot straps to gain fortune and position—but to recapture the woman who is his life, he is going to have to change. TOUGH GUY, SAVVY LADY will touch you deeply . . . and joyfully.

Little could be so rare as being trapped IN A GOLDEN WEB, Courtney Henke's LOVESWEPT #476. Heroine Elizabeth Hammer is desperate! Framed for a crime she didn't commit, she's driven to actions she never dreamed she was capable of taking. And kidnapping gorgeous hunk Dexter Wolffe and forcing him to take her to Phoenix is just the start. Dex plays along—finding the beautiful bank manager the most delectable adversary he's ever encountered. He wants to kiss her defiant mouth and make her his prisoner . . . of love. You'll thrill to the romance of these two loners on the lam in one of LOVESWEPT's most delightful offerings ever!

And a dozen American beauties to Glenna McReynolds for her fabulously inventive OUTLAW CARSON, LOVESWEPT #478. We'll wager you've never run into a hero like Kit Carson before. Heroine Kristine Richards certainly hasn't. When the elusive, legendary Kit shows up at her university, Kristine can only wonder if he's a smuggler, a scholar—or a blessing from heaven, sent to shatter her senses. Kit is shocked by Kristine . . . for he had never believed before meeting her that there was any woman on earth who could arouse in him such fierce hunger . . . or such desperate jealousy. Both are burdened with secrets and wary of each other and have a long and difficult labyrinth to struggle through. But there are glimpses ahead of a Shangri-la just for them! As dramatic and surprising as a budding rose in winter, OUTLAW CARSON will enchant you!

Welcome to Tonya Wood who makes her debut with us with a real charmer in LOVESWEPT #477, GORGEOUS. Sam Christie was just too good-looking to be real. And too talented. And women were always throwing themselves at him. Well, until Mercy Rose Sullivan appeared in his life. When Mercy rescues Sam from the elevator in their apartment building, he can't believe what an endearing gypsy she is—or that she doesn't recognize him! Mercy is as feisty as she is guileless and puts up a terrific fight against Sam's long, slow, deep kisses. His fame is driving them apart just as love is bursting into full bloom . . . and it seems that only a miracle can bring these two dreamers together, where they belong. Sheer magical romance!

What is more perfect to read about on a perfect day than a long, lean, mean deputy sheriff and a lady locksmith who's been called to free him from the bed he is handcuffed to? Nothing! So run to pick-up your copy of SILVER BRACELETS, LOVE-SWEPT #479, by Sandra Chastain. You'll laugh and cry and root for these two unlikely lovers to get together. Sarah Wilson is as tenderhearted as they come. Asa Canyon is one rough, tough hombre who has always been determined to stay free of emotional entanglements. They taste ecstasy together . . . but is Sarah brave enough to risk loving such a man? And can Asa dare to believe that a woman will always be there for him? A romance as vivid and fresh and thrilling as a crimson rose!

And don't forget FANFARE next month with its irresistible longer fiction.

First, STORM WINDS by Iris Johansen. This thrilling, sweeping novel set against the turbulent times of the French Revolution continues with stories of those whose lives are touched by the fabled Wind Dancer. Two unforgettable pairs of lovers will have you singing the praises of Iris Johansen all summer long! DREAMS TO KEEP by Nomi Berger is a powerfully moving novel of a memorable and courageous woman, a survivor of the Warsaw ghetto, who defies all odds and builds a life and a fortune in America. But she is a woman who will risk everything for revenge on the man who condemned her family . . . until a love that is larger than life itself gives her a vision of a future of which she'd never dreamed. And all you LOVESWEPT readers will know you have to be sure to get a copy of MAGIC by Tami Hoag in which the fourth of the "fearsome foursome" gets a love for all time. This utterly enchanting love story shows off the best of Tami Hoag! Remember, FANFARE signals that something great is coming. . . .

Enjoy your perfect days to come with perfect reading from LOVESWEPT and FANFARE!

With every good wish,

Carolyn Nichols

Carolyn Nichols
Editor
LOVESWEPT
Bantam Books
666 Fifth Avenue
New York, NY 10103

THE LATEST IN BOOKS AND AUDIO CASSETTES